SARAH'S LEGACY

SARAH'S LEGACY

Valerie Sherrard

A BOARDWALK BOOK
A MEMBER OF THE DUNDURN GROUP
TORONTO

Editor: Barry Jowett
Copy-Editor: Jennifer Gallant
Design: Jennifer Scott
Printer: Webcom

National Library of Canada Cataloguing in Publication Data

Sherrard, Valerie
    Sarah's legacy / Valerie Sherrard.

ISBN-10: 1-55002-602-X
ISBN-13: 978-1-55002-602-3
    I. Title.

PS8587.H3867S27 2006   jC813'.6   C2006-900508-7

1   2   3   4   5   10   09   08   07   06

Conseil des Arts du Canada   Canada Council for the Arts   Canada   ONTARIO ARTS COUNCIL CONSEIL DES ARTS DE L'ONTARIO

We acknowledge the support of the **Canada Council for the Arts** and the **Ontario Arts Council** for our publishing program. We also acknowledge the financial support of the **Government of Canada** through the **Book Publishing Industry Development Program** and **The Association for the Export of Canadian Books**, and the **Government of Ontario** through the **Ontario Book Publishers Tax Credit** program, and the **Ontario Media Development Corporation.**

Care has been taken to trace the ownership of copyright material used in this book. The author and the publisher welcome any information enabling them to rectify any references or credits in subsequent editions.

J. Kirk Howard, President

Printed and bound in Canada.

www.dundurn.com

Dundurn Press
3 Church Street, Suite 500
Toronto, Ontario, Canada
M5E 1M2

Gazelle Book Services Limited
White Cross Mills
High Town, Lancaster, England
LA1 4XS

Dundurn Press
2250 Military Road
Tonawanda, NY
U.S.A. 14150

To Mom and Dad with much love

I pause to think of years gone by
(A child can't know how time will fly)
And moments that will never fade
That live in memory's parade.

The many times Dad read to me
Those wondrous words of poetry
(Of moo cow moos and master's hands)
Transporting me to made-up lands.

And Mom, in endless, countless ways
You cared for me through childhood days
You mended clothes and hearts and knees
And taught me so much — patiently!

Within my heart to hold, to stay
The gold remains. The dross? Away!
What live — and shall live ever after
Are memories of love and laughter.

ACKNOWLEDGEMENTS

Parents who read to their children give them something that cannot be equalled by any other means. My parents, Bob and Pauline Russell, to whom this book is dedicated, shared their love of poetry and literature with my brothers, Danny and Andrew, and me from the time we could barely walk. Some of my fondest childhood memories are centred around stories and poems, and I can still hear their voices, one soft, one deep, but both delivering the words with feeling and passion. For their love and support, then and now, I thank them. For many other things, I thank:

My husband, partner, and best friend, Brent.

My son, Anthony, his wife, Maria, and daughter, Emilee. My daughter, Pamela, and her fiancé, David Jardine. My brothers and their families: Danny and Gail;

Andrew, Shelley, and Bryce. My "other" family: Ron and Phoebe Sherrard, Ron Sherrard and Dr. Kiran Pure, Bruce and Roxanne Mullin, and Karen Sherrard.

Friends: Janet Aube, Jimmy Allain, Karen Arseneault, Dawn Black, Karen Donovan, Angi Garofolo, John Hambrook, Sandra Henderson, Jim Hennessy, Alf Lower, Mary Matchett, Johnnye Montgomery, Marsha Skrypuch, Linda Stevens, Ashley Smith, Pam Sturgeon, and Bonnie Thompson.

At The Dundurn Group: Kirk Howard, Publisher, as well as very special thanks to some of the awesome team: my editor, Barry Jowett; director of design, Jennifer Scott; and assistant editor Jennifer Gallant.

My fabulous agent: Leona Trainer of Transatlantic Literary Agency.

Teenagers! Hearing from you is the *best* part of writing, and I love getting your letters and emails. In recent months, the following readers have taken the time to get in touch: Avalon Borg, Victoria Briggs, Laura Graziano, Melissa Harms, Vanessa Hesse, Samantha-Louise Landry, Samantha Lo, Andrea Lucchese, Chelsea Purdy, Bailey Tait, Kelisha Villafana, and Veronica Williston. Also, Fiona To has shared many words, as well as work that holds tremendous promise.

You are on these pages and they belong to you.

CHAPTER ONE

You know how it is when you get a feeling that something big is going to happen? Like when you wake up in the morning and everything inside you somehow *knows* that there's a good thing coming, and then you find out that your essay won a pizza party for your class, or your best friend invites you to her family's cottage for a whole week, or something else really cool happens.

Well, it wasn't like that for me. In fact, that Thursday started out like any other day.

I had a bowl of cereal for breakfast, made a sandwich for lunch, and headed off to school. The day passed as normal as you please, with nothing out of the ordinary at all.

I checked the mail on my way in from school that afternoon. I always did that, seeing as I got home before

Mom. She worked over at Pete's Diner and didn't get home until after seven. Some days it was even later. She always brought our supper home in a brown paper bag. Usually it was the special of the day. Sometimes they ran out of the special and we had hotdogs and fries or, if the tips had been really good that day, a piece of chicken. Whatever it was, it was always almost cold because the diner was a fifteen-minute walk from our apartment. But by then I'd be hungry enough not to care, even if I'd had a snack after school.

Anyway, I was mentioning the mail. I never paid much attention to it, although I knew some people did. They probably got more interesting mail than we did. We never got any mail worth getting excited over. At least, we didn't before this particular day. Mostly, the only thing we got was bills. Mom tried to look cheerful when she opened them. She'd usually say something like, "Well, this isn't too bad. We can pay this." Once in a while, though, she didn't say anything and she couldn't quite hide the worry. Then I knew not to ask for money for a Saturday matinee or any of the other little extras that we could usually afford.

On this Thursday, there was a letter for Mom. I hardly glanced at it before I put it on top of the fridge, except to see that it had some kind of business return label in the corner and that Mom's name and address were typed. I figured that meant it was probably a bill of some sort. I hoped it wasn't an overdue notice. We got those once in a while and they always upset Mom.

I guess most people would consider us poor. Well, I suppose we were, in a way. But we had enough to eat and a place to live. Mom always said that if you had those two things you were doing okay. She said there were more important things in life than fancy houses and cars and stuff and I guess she was right. Still, there were times when I wished I had some of the things other kids at school had.

Most of all, though, I wished that my mom didn't have to work long shifts at Pete's Diner. She worked six days a week but Pete didn't pay her any overtime. He said he could always get someone else to work the extra hours at regular pay if she didn't like it. I guess that was true, but it's hard to see your mom tired all the time and looking a lot older than her thirty-four years.

When she got home that evening everything was still going along the way it always did. She brought Styrofoam bowls with chili and thick slices of whole wheat bread and we sat at the table to eat. It was wobbling a little, like it always did, because the floor wasn't even and one leg didn't quite touch.

Mom asked me about my day at school and I asked her about work. She didn't eat much of her supper, which was pretty normal too. She always said that after looking at food all day her appetite was gone.

Our television hadn't been working since about a month before, when it had just died in the middle of *Corner Gas*. Mom thought it was the picture tube and she figured it would cost more to fix it than the set was worth. We'd started a TV fund, but I wasn't expecting we'd get another one anytime soon. We had a cookie jar, the old-fashioned kind, and we'd put spare money into it when we were saving up for something special. Somehow, other things always came up and we had to borrow from the jar. Well, we called it borrowing, but the jar never seemed to get paid back.

I didn't care much about the TV. Most evenings I did my homework and read for a while, or Mom and I sat around and played rummy and crib and just talked. That night was no different.

We'd gotten out the crib board and cut the deck to see who'd have the first crib hand. Low card always wins that, and I'd cut a three to Mom's seven, so it was my turn to deal. I was just shuffling the cards when I remembered the envelope for Mom.

"Oh, I almost forgot," I said. "There's a letter for you." I jumped up and fetched it from the top of the fridge, hoping it wasn't anything that would upset Mom. Then she might not feel like playing cards. I passed it to her and sat back down, waiting.

She looked at the return address for a minute and her face got puzzled and a bit worried.

"This is from a lawyer's office," she said slowly, sliding her fingernail under the flap and tearing it open. "What could it be about?"

It was the kind of question that isn't looking for an answer so I stayed quiet, feeling almost angry at whoever had sent the letter. We sure didn't need any bad news.

Mom's mouth was moving then, the way it does when she reads something to herself. Sometimes I'd try to read her lips but this time I just sat there crossing my fingers. I've never found that this helps, but I still did it just in case.

"My great-aunt Sarah passed away," Mom announced when she was partway through the letter. Her shoulders kind of sagged with relief and I thought maybe crossing my fingers had finally worked. Not that I thought someone dying was good news or anything, but it was better than an overdue notice we couldn't pay. And I couldn't remember ever hearing of this aunt before, so it was pretty hard to feel sad.

"Sarah?" I asked, curious because that's also my name. "Am I named after her?"

"Yes and no," Mom said distractedly. I hate it when she says that, like it's supposed to tell me something. I said nothing, though, because she was reading again and the expression on her face was changing. "Wait," she said, "that's not all." Pink spots appeared in her cheeks and she looked shocked.

"I can't believe it," she said.

CHAPTER TWO

"What is it?" I asked anxiously. Mom looked dazed, which made her face hard to read. I couldn't tell if the news in the rest of the letter was good or bad.

"Wait," she said in a hushed voice. She was reading the letter again, as if she wasn't sure she'd really understood what it said. When she finished going through it for the second time her fingers loosened and it fluttered to the table. Her hands were trembling.

"Oh, Sarah!" she whispered. I wasn't sure if she was talking to me or referring to her great-aunt. Either way I was getting a bit impatient to know what it was all about. Then Mom took a deep breath and looked across the table at me. It seemed as if she was having a hard time focusing her eyes, the way she stared almost without seeing me.

"My aunt," she began in a faltering voice, "has left us everything. Everything."

"You mean money?" The first thought that came to me was that Mom wouldn't have to work all those long shifts anymore. Then, I had a vision of us being rich and me being able to have all kinds of things we could never afford now. I felt a twinge of guilt for thinking so quickly about what *I* was going to get out of it.

"It sounds as if there's some money," Mom answered, "though I don't know how much. But the big thing is her estate. She's left us her home and all its contents. And her pets."

"Her pets?"

"Apparently there's a variety, though it doesn't say exactly what. Probably a cat and dog or something. One of the conditions of the will is that we take care of them."

"How will we get them here?"

"We won't. That's the other condition." Mom seemed to be working things out in her head and took a minute to continue. "In order to inherit the property, we have to live in the house at least until you complete your education. After that we're free to sell it if we want to."

I thought that was kind of weird, then realized there was a lot more at stake than this aunt's oddities. "Where is it?" I asked quickly.

"A small city in New Brunswick called Miramichi."

VALERIE SHERRARD

"Never heard of it," I said, as if I could wish the place away like that. "Anyway, I don't want to live in New Brunswick. I like Ontario."

Mom looked cross then and told me I was being selfish. I could feel a lecture coming and I was right. She told me that this was a chance for us to have a house and for her not to have to kill herself working just to keep us going and there I was complaining at the idea of moving. Still, we'd lived in Ontario my whole life and the thought of going somewhere else made my stomach feel kind of sick.

"But all my friends are here," I said sullenly. "I don't want to move."

"I see," Mom said. Her lips had gone into a thin line, which always means she's really angry. "So, you want me to write to this lawyer and tell her we don't want the house?"

"I didn't mean that," I said, though I could see how it sounded as if that was exactly what I'd meant. "But I don't understand why we can't find a way around that part. If she left the place to us we should be allowed to do what we want with it."

"As I've already told you, there are two conditions to the inheritance. One is that we live there, the other is that we take care of Sarah's pets. If we aren't prepared to do that, the house is to be sold and the money from the sale will be used to provide for the pets. When none of them are living, the remaining funds will go to a charity."

"That's stupid. It sounds like she cares more about her dumb animals than she does about us. Why'd she bother leaving us anything if that's how she felt?"

"Well, Sarah, I imagine she loved her pets. Perhaps they were her only companions. But she obviously cared about us, too, or she wouldn't have left us her house. Do you think we were ever going to have a home of our own on the money I make as a waitress?"

"I guess not." It was starting to sink in. We were going to be moving, all right. I can't say I was happy about it.

"Our own house," Mom said. She had a faraway look on her face and seemed to be talking to herself again. "I wonder what it's like."

"You've never been there?"

"I've never even met my great-aunt," Mom answered. "I remember seeing pictures of her at my grandfather's house, though. It seems she was something of a recluse."

"What's that?"

"A recluse? Someone who doesn't like to be around other people. I vaguely recall hearing the story of how she went to New Brunswick when she was around twenty, which was quite a thing for a woman on her own in those days. I don't think anyone ever saw her again after that. The only contact was an occasional letter."

This aunt was sounding more and more like a weirdo, if you ask me. I could picture her, old and alone, petting her stupid animals and talking to herself.

"I don't care where she went or what she did," I said, "she doesn't have the right to force people to live somewhere they don't want to go."

"Now, Sarah. This is hardly the worst thing in the world, you know. You might even like living in New Brunswick."

"I'll hate it," I said firmly. I added "and I hate her" to that, but only in my head.

"I'm afraid you're going to have to get used to the idea, and fast." Mom sighed and stood up. "I'll be calling the lawyer tomorrow and making arrangements. If everything goes well, we should be moving by the end of next week."

It hadn't occurred to me that we'd be leaving so soon. I mumbled something about waiting until the end of the school year, which was a few months away, but Mom just gave me a look. It was one of those looks that tell you there's not going to be any more discussion on the matter.

I stomped off to my room and lay on the bed sulking. The more I thought about the whole thing, the angrier I got. What gave this old woman we'd never even met the right to decide where we were going to live? It wasn't fair!

Mom came in later to say good night but I pretended I was already asleep.

CHAPTER THREE

I tried to keep sulking over the weekend but it was just about impossible. Mom was all excited and happy and some of her attitude started rubbing off on me. She'd quit her job as soon as she'd talked to the lawyer and was flitting around packing and singing little snatches of songs. After hearing her talk about our move as some kind of fun adventure, I was starting to feel a bit differently about it.

I found I was looking at our apartment a lot differently, too. It had seemed okay before, but now it was starting to look pretty shabby. My room, with its worn carpet and its yellow rose–patterned wallpaper that was cracked in several places, suddenly seemed uglier than I'd ever noticed.

The whole place was dingy and badly decorated. It was easy to see that the landlord had bought whatever was on sale when he was choosing flooring and wall coverings, regardless of whether anything matched or not. I wasn't sorry to be moving out of the dreary place we'd called home for the last three years.

Saying goodbye to my friends was going to be the hardest thing. Mom pointed out that we could probably afford a computer once we got settled into our new place, and then I could keep in touch with everyone by email. It was a small consolation, but at least it was something.

It was all happening so fast that I hardly had time to think. We had a lot to do, deciding what to take and what to sell or give away before we left. Mom made up handwritten signs advertising everything that was too big to take along, and before I knew it our beds were sold. We slept on the floor the last few nights, which wasn't nearly as uncomfortable as I'd expected.

There were a few things left by Wednesday of the next week and Mom called a goodwill organization that sent a truck around to pick it all up. We spent that night in a hotel since we no longer even had blankets or pillows and the power had been turned off in our apartment.

I'd been hoping we might fly to New Brunswick, since I've never been on a plane. Money was too tight, though, and the cost of tickets was more than we could afford. Instead we boarded the train early Thursday afternoon and settled in for the overnight ride.

"It was a lucky thing that this came along so close to the end of the month," Mom said as we ate a light meal in the dining car late in the day. "I don't know how we'd have managed the trip if I didn't have the rent money for April put aside. As it is, we're going to have to watch every cent until things are settled."

"Can't we move right into the house?"

"I don't know. But I'm sure we'll manage until the legal business is all taken care of."

That got me thinking. What if something went wrong and we were left without anywhere to go for a while? Even with the rent money and what we'd made from selling our furniture, we only had a few hundred dollars left after we'd paid for the hotel and train tickets.

Mom seemed optimistic, though, so I decided not to worry about it. Back in our seats, I soon found that the darkness outside and the steady rocking motion of the train made me sleepy.

The next thing I knew I was waking up, startled to see a man in a blue uniform standing beside me. It took a few seconds before I remembered where we were. Mom was already awake and she smiled as I blinked and looked around.

"Almost there," she said cheerfully. "I have your toiletry bag ready so you can tidy up before we get to Miramichi."

It's not easy to brush your teeth while the train is swaying back and forth but I managed it. I washed my face and combed my hair, too, scowling at what I saw in the mirror. I've never been too happy with the way I look. Mom says that's normal for girls my age. She insists that I'm pretty, but then, she *is* my mom.

I don't look much like my mother. Sometimes someone will say we look alike, but I don't see it. My hair is dark brown while hers is fawn coloured, and her skin is lighter than mine. My lips are a lot fuller than hers, too. Sometimes she jokes that I was born pouting, because my bottom lip is so full it seems to stick out.

I guess I look more like my father, though it's a bit hard to tell from looking at the few pictures we have of him. Mom always says he was the most handsome man she ever saw. His name was Shane Gilmore and he'd come to Canada from Ireland three years before Mom met him.

She was working in a coffee shop and he started dropping in on his way home from his job with a construction company. After he'd been going there for a few months he asked her out and she broke her rule of never dating customers.

"I was so taken with him, his good looks and charm," she told me often, reliving the happy time in her life when she'd been in love. "Shane loved excitement and we went to a lot of places that I'd never gone before. It was a whole new world for me."

When they'd been seeing each other for about half a year, he asked her to marry him. Mom says that was the happiest day of her life, up until I was born.

"Your grandparents didn't approve of Shane." She'd frown, remembering. "They thought he was a bit too wild. But they were wrong. It's true that he liked to have fun but he was a good man."

Then, only seventeen short days after their wedding, there was an accident. I never got a lot of details because Mom didn't like to talk about it. All I know is that my father was hit by a driver who was high on something. He died three days later.

Mom still gets upset when she talks about that. It must have been so horrible. One day she was a brand new bride and the next thing she knew she was standing beside her husband's coffin.

A few weeks later Mom found out that she was going to have a baby. Me. It really makes me sad that my dad never knew anything about me. Not even that I was going to be born.

As a young child, I used to pretend that my father might come to the door one day and explain that it had somehow all been a terrible mistake. Of course I knew that was never really going to happen. I'd given up that fantasy years ago.

Well, there was no sense dwelling on any of this now. I made my way back to our seats just as the train was pulling into the station.

Chapter Four

My first impression of Miramichi wasn't all that great. Mom had told me it was a city, so I was expecting something a lot different than the small town we'd just left in Ontario. But from the train station, which was on a hill overlooking the place, I could see right off that it wasn't very big. There were no skyscrapers to be seen, just a bunch of houses on either side of the tracks.

"Are you sure this is the right place?" I asked Mom. "It sure doesn't look like a city." We'd been to Toronto a few times and I'd imagined our new home would look something like that, only on a smaller scale.

"This is it, all right." Mom took my hand then, as if I were going to get lost in the big crowd of about twenty people. "Let's get our luggage."

I followed along, trying unsuccessfully to tug my hand away from her. It's kind of embarrassing to have your mom holding your hand when you're twelve years old.

The luggage she'd referred to was an old set of four battered suitcases that stood out among the others on the cart. Once we'd picked them up Mom went to call a taxi.

The driver was a small old man who looked bored. He asked, "Where to?" without any sign of interest and seemed annoyed when Mom didn't answer right away.

"We'd like an inexpensive place to stay for the night," she said at last.

"Yeah? There's a hotel not far from here, pretty cheap." He glanced in the rear-view mirror questioningly. "Wanna go there?"

"That will be fine."

A few minutes later we were deposited at a hotel and Mom arranged for a room.

"Well, then," she said brightly, in a way that told me she was forcing herself to be enthusiastic, "first we'll shower, change, and get some breakfast. That will leave us the whole day to go exploring and see what we can accomplish."

I felt a bit better once my hair was washed and I had clean clothes on. When Mom was ready too, we went for a walk and found a restaurant called the Goodie Shop.

A friendly waitress served us bacon and eggs. Mom asked her about the street we needed to find.

"Wellington Street? That's over in Chatham."

"I understood it was in Miramichi," Mom said, confused.

"It is, only most folks still call it Chatham. You're not from around here, huh? Chatham, Newcastle, Douglastown, and all the small places around here became Miramichi a few years back."

That explained things! We hadn't moved to a city at all, just a bunch of towns that had been joined together.

"Where are we now?" Mom inquired.

"This here's Newcastle. To get to Chatham, you have to cross the river and take a left at the lights. Or you can use the new highway if you want, but the Morrisey Bridge is closer from here." She pointed in the general direction.

"We don't have a car," Mom sighed. "I was hoping we could walk there."

The waitress startled us by turning and yelling to a man seated alone at a table across the room. "Hey, Stan, you going to Chatham?"

"Yep." He smiled and nodded vigorously.

"Give these folks a lift over, would you? They're going to Wellington Street."

"No problem." He turned his nodding, smiling face toward us. "Let me know when you're ready. No hurry."

Mom looked like she wanted to protest but couldn't think of anything to say. I knew she felt dumb to be bumming a ride from a stranger. Still, we couldn't be throwing around the little money we had left on taxis. As it was, we'd need to hire a cab to get back to our hotel.

About ten minutes later, Stan led us to his car and we were on our way. As we drove, he asked a bunch of questions about where we were from. Mom seemed a bit put out by his inquisitive nature but she answered politely.

"So, you've moved here. That's great, then." He nodded approvingly, as if we'd done something wonderful. "And you're staying in Newcastle for now, are you?"

Mom allowed that we were.

"What time will you be heading back, then?"

"I, we, I really don't know. We were going to take a look around for a bit."

"Right." He smiled and his head bobbed up and down again. "Well, I'll be going back to Newcastle this afternoon. Be glad to meet you somewhere and give you a lift if you're ready around three."

"I'm not sure…" Mom's voice trailed off.

"Tell you what. See this here corner store?" He motioned at a Petro Canada station. "I'll swing by at three and if you're here I'll take you back to Newcastle. Now, whereabouts were you needing to go on Wellington?"

Mom recited the address.

"Just up the road a bit." For a few seconds there was silence as Stan looked at house numbers. Then he pulled the car over, announcing, "Here we are."

"Thank you so very much."

"Don't mention it." He was squinting at the house we were in front of. "Say, that's old Sarah Wentworth's house, isn't it?"

"Yes, it is." Mom stepped out of the car quickly, clearly wanting to avoid any more questions. "Thank you again."

"No trouble." Stan smiled and waved as he drove away. It was only after he'd gone that we turned to really look at the house.

A moment passed, then another. Both of our mouths had fallen open, but neither of us spoke right off. The place was enormous! Pillars stood on either side of the cement steps leading up to the door. The entrance was set back in the centre between two sections, each graced by a large bay window. Four more windows looked out from the upstairs and beyond that two smaller ones peeked out from what must have been a third floor or an attic.

I found my voice first.

"Are you sure this is the right place?"

"It has to be." Mom sounded as unconvinced as I felt. "The address is right and the man who drove us here even knew it had belonged to Aunt Sarah."

When I could move, I walked to the side, where a driveway led to another door on the right of the house. Beyond that entrance, there was what appeared to be another small house attached to the main one. It too had its own door.

A sudden movement in one of the windows startled me. I jumped, thinking someone was inside and that they'd wonder what we were doing, gawking at the place. A nervous giggle escaped when I saw a furry face peering out.

"Just a dumb old cat," I said aloud. Then I realized that this was *our* cat now and I felt a bit guilty for calling it dumb. Mom wandered off around the back of the place as I stood watching the cat lick its paw and rub the side of its face.

"Hey!" shouted a voice, tearing my attention away from the cat. "What are you doing here?"

When I turned, I saw a boy who looked to be a few years older than me. He was staring at me in a way that suggested he thought I was some kind of criminal planning to rob the place. His tone had been so harsh that I couldn't find my voice right away. Before I could answer, he spoke again.

"You can't hang around here."

"Says who?"

"Says me." He took a step forward. "I'm taking care of the place."

"Yeah? Well, my mother and I are the new owners," I announced haughtily.

"No kidding? Why didn't you say so in the first place?" He smiled then. "I guess I sort of scared you, huh?"

"You did not," I denied, even though it was true he'd frightened me for a moment.

"Anyway, I'm David Murray. We live a couple of houses down." His head jerked to the left. I assumed that meant he lived in that direction.

"I'm Sarah Gilmore." Seeing Mom coming back, I added, "And this is my mother."

Mom put her hand out and he shook it awkwardly, introducing himself again.

"I've been taking care of Sarah's animals and checking on the place and stuff. I just came over to put out food and walk the dogs. Have you been inside yet?"

We told him we hadn't. He produced a key.

"I guess you'd like to have a look around, then."

We followed him eagerly, totally unprepared for what we were about to see!

CHAPTER FIVE

As soon as the door swung closed behind us and David flicked on the light, three cats and a small dog appeared at his side, jumping, rubbing against his legs, and starting up a chorus of mews and barks. David went immediately into a room off the large kitchen we'd entered and started getting out cans and boxes of food.

"Four animals," I observed, watching as he leaned down to fill bowls that were out of my view. "No, five," I added as a larger dog hurried by.

"More," Mom's voice was barely a whisper. Her mouth was hanging open.

She was right. Another cat ran past, then a pair of dogs followed by a final cat.

"There can't be *nine* pets," I said finally.

"Nine pets," Mom echoed hollowly.

"There are eleven, actually," David called from the next room. "There's a parrot — an African grey that talks named Stoolie. And, uh, there's Rosie. She's a skunk."

"A skunk," Mom said faintly. She looked as though she might have gone into shock.

"Yeah, Rosie is pretty much nocturnal so you don't see her around much in the daytime. There are special instructions for her diet and stuff in a notebook here." He opened a drawer near the sink and drew out a small coil book with a picture of a skunk pasted on the cover.

"A skunk," Mom said. "Eleven animals!" She repeated both things several times and then sank onto a nearby chair and stared straight ahead. I couldn't help wondering what she thought of her great-aunt at that moment.

"A few of them are pretty old," David said helpfully.

I walked to the doorway to see if, as I suspected, he was smiling. He was.

"They're all personalized," he said, waving his hand toward the gobbling creatures in the room.

"What, the cats and dogs?" I was confused.

"No, their dishes. They each have two. One for food and one for water." He leaned down and picked up a bowl to show me. On the side of it the word "Inky" appeared between black paw prints.

"Don't worry about trying to make them eat from their own dishes, though." His smile was growing. "I just let them go to the nearest bowl."

I frowned. His amusement was not contagious.

"Wait till you see downstairs." He was actually laughing by this time. "The cats' litter boxes are personalized too. And the skunk's. And I might as well tell you right now that hers has to be in the same place all the time. Skunks pick out a favourite place to 'go' and that's that. Hard to believe, huh?"

He was wrong. I'd have believed just about anything right then. But for Mom, the mention of six litter boxes was too much. A gasp, followed by a short, strangled cry came out of her. It seemed to restore her, though, because she got up then and joined us.

"This is a pantry," she said indignantly. "Or, at least, it was *meant* to be one."

David shrugged. "You can move their dishes somewhere else if you want, I guess. I don't think they're particular about where they eat."

Mom stared at him blankly, but a sudden high-pitched cry of "*Knock it off!*" from down the hallway startled her back to awareness.

"That's Stoolie," David explained. "He's *always* telling someone to knock it off — and saying other bossy things. Anyway, did you want to have a look through the house now? I have to get back home to watch my kid brother when my dad goes to work."

We did a quick tour, trying to push aside the thought

that our inheritance included this unbelievable menagerie of pets.

Stoolie told us to knock it off again as we passed him. He also commanded us to feed the pretty bird, though his dish was brimming.

I have to say that the house was beautiful. There were two rooms off the kitchen, the pantry we'd already seen, and what David referred to as the back kitchen. Who ever heard of a house having two kitchens?

Most of the floors were hardwood and a lot of the furniture was fancy-looking wood stuff too. A fire-place stood in what David called the sitting room downstairs. I'd never heard the names he used for some of the rooms before, being used to a kitchen, living room, bedrooms, and a bathroom, though of course I'd heard of dining rooms, too. But our house contained rooms that David referred to as a parlour and a den. Upstairs there were four enormous bed-rooms and two smaller rooms that David identified as a sewing room and a quiet room. Two of the bed-rooms also had fireplaces.

"You can check out the attic another time," he told us, gesturing toward a square set into the ceiling of the upstairs hallway. "This is the entry to it. A ladder comes down when you open it."

"What's the other building attached at the back of the house?" I asked when we'd gone through the place.

"Used to be servants' quarters," he said, "but Sarah used it for storing things. There are two entrances to it, one outside and one from the back kitchen, but both are kept locked. The lawyer will have the keys for those doors."

I'd never heard of servants' quarters. Mom explained that years ago very rich people had wings built on their homes for the hired help to live in.

"You seem to have known my great-aunt quite well," Mom remarked to David.

"I helped her out when she needed something done. She was a nice old lady." He looked away then and I could see that he felt sad about her dying. It was weird that we were her family and we didn't even know her or feel particularly bad that she'd died, but this person who was no relation to her did.

Before we left the house, David gave Mom a slip of paper with his phone number on it. "You'll probably need a hand when you move in," he explained, not realizing that all we had was four suitcases with our clothes.

"I guess we'll have to find out the pets' names," Mom sighed, tucking the paper into her purse. "All eleven of them."

"Where are we going now?" I asked as we stepped back out onto the sidewalk.

"The lawyer's office is apparently nearby," Mom said. "She told me when I spoke to her that it was only a few minutes' walk from Sarah's house. We have an appointment with her right after lunch."

We found the place, which was in a house that had been converted to lawyers' offices. Five names appeared on a sign hanging above the door, and our lawyer, Nicole Standing, was listed among them.

Neither of us was hungry after a late breakfast, so to kill time until our appointment we just walked around for a while. Not too far from Aunt Sarah's house there was a nice little park and we sat on a bench there for a bit. In one corner of the park was a low, red brick build- ing, which we discovered was the library. I thought it was a bonus that the library was so close. I like to read but we've never been able to afford books. Or, at least, we couldn't before.

A young woman ushered us right into the lawyer's office when we returned there for our appointment. Ms. Standing stood to greet us, shook our hands, and told us she was sorry about our loss. That confused me for a second until I realized she was talking about Aunt Sarah's death. Mom thanked her solemnly.

"It took a little while to locate you," Ms. Standing told us, "which gave me time to get everything pretty well in order. We'll just get this paperwork out of the way and then you can go ahead and take possession of your home."

"Today?" Mom asked.

"Well, not quite that fast, but I'd say by Monday. Where are you staying in the meantime, in case I need to contact you?"

Mom gave her the name of the hotel. She sounded worried. Then Ms. Standing looked at her closely and asked if we were all right for money.

"I guess we can manage for a few days," Mom said, but her voice was unconvincing. I knew that four nights in a hotel, plus meals, would cost more than what we had left but she didn't want to admit that.

"Well, let's just make things a bit simpler." Ms. Standing pressed a button on her desk and a moment later the receptionist appeared.

"Angela, would you call the Gilmores' hotel and have them bill their room to my office?" Then she assured Mom it was no problem and she'd just add the cost to her bill.

"Your bill," Mom echoed, looking very uncomfortable. "Will it be very much?"

"Don't worry about that." She smiled. "It will just come off the money that's been left to you, along with the house."

"You haven't clarified that, I mean, how much money is actually involved?"

"Of course, I won't have an exact figure for you until everything is settled," Ms. Standing said. She was smiling, which was no wonder since she was about to deliver very good news. "I can tell you, however, that it will be somewhere in the neighbourhood of thirty-seven thousand dollars."

Mom started to cry.

CHAPTER SIX

Thirty-seven thousand dollars! After all the years of watching every penny, it sounded like a million to us. When we left Ms. Standing's office we were both practically in shock. We walked slowly along Wellington Street, stopped to admire our house again, and then went back toward the park. Every so far we paused and looked at each other and said that we couldn't believe it. That wasn't quite true; we did believe it, but it was going to take a while to totally sink in.

"Are we rich?" I asked as we went by the park.

"Not by a long shot. But it will certainly keep us going until I can find work. Still, we'll have to be careful with it just the same."

"Will we get a car?" We'd never had a car and I'd always thought how wonderful it would be to be able to go wherever you wanted whenever you wanted to.

"Yes, we'll have a car. And you'll have a computer."

As we continued walking I couldn't help thinking that a few weeks ago all of these things would have seemed impossible. We'd managed on so little for so long that it was going to be hard to get used to having things.

"There's one thing I can't figure out. Why did Aunt Sarah leave everything to me?" Mom wondered aloud, breaking into my thoughts. "I can't understand it. There are lots of kin she could have named as her heirs."

That *was* kind of puzzling. It's not as though we were closer to her than the others. We didn't even know her! I wondered if any of her relatives had ever visited or written to her or anything. Then an idea popped into my head.

"Maybe it's because she thought I was named after her," I suggested.

"You could be right. I hadn't even thought of that. But I guess we'll never know for sure."

"Hi gals, how's she going?" a man's voice called from across the street.

When we looked over, we saw that the odd greeting had come from Stan, who had pulled his car up to the curb opposite to where we were standing.

"Oh, hello." Mom gave a little wave.

"I was just driving along when I spied the two of you." He nodded as if to prove what he was saying was true. "How'd you make out? Did you like what you saw of Chatham?"

"It seems very nice."

"Good then, great." More nodding. "If you're ready to go back to Newcastle, I'm on my way there now."

Mom hesitated for a second and then told him it would be much appreciated. We crossed the street and climbed into the car. We'd hardly pulled away from the curb when Stan asked a question that surprised us both.

"I guess you must be the pair who've inherited old Sarah Wentworth's place, then, are you?"

"We are," Mom said in surprise. "How did you know that?"

"Ah, you can't keep nothing secret around here."

"Anything," Mom said automatically. I almost burst out laughing and just kept it in by taking a deep breath and holding it. Mom is so used to correcting my grammar that she sometimes slips and does it with other people too.

"Huh?" Stan had missed her meaning.

"Oh, don't pay me any mind. I was just thinking out loud." Mom gave me a warning look that suggested I keep my amusement under control. "Anyway, how was it that you heard we'd inherited my great-aunt's estate?"

Rather than being embarrassed about admitting that he'd been listening to gossip about us, Stan seemed proud to have gotten the information. He launched into an explanation of how he'd been talking to someone who'd heard it from a neighbour who, in turn, had gotten the news from someone else. It sounded as if all the details of our lives had been passed about and discussed by the whole city. And we'd been there for less than six hours!

"I see," Mom said coldly. Almost anyone should have been able to tell that she was annoyed to find herself the centre of so much attention from people she didn't even know. Not Stan, though. He beamed and went on about how he'd put two and two together and concluded that we were the ones moving into the Wentworth house. I thought his pride over it was a bit ridiculous. After all, he'd dropped us off there that morning; it wouldn't take a towering genius to figure out that we were the folks inheriting the place.

It wasn't long before he switched from boasting about his powers of deduction to fishing for information. Mom was deliberately vague when she replied to anything he asked and I could see he was disappointed that he wasn't getting any juicy details about us. I suppose the fact that he'd met us gave him a place of importance among the gossips and he was keen to have something interesting to add to the circulating stories. Well, he didn't get anything from Mom!

She was obviously relieved to get away from his questions when we got back to the part of Miramichi that locals still called Newcastle. He offered to take us right to wherever we were staying but Mom is too cautious for that. Instead of letting him know what hotel we were at, she told him to drop us off downtown.

"We'll look around a bit and get some dinner first," she said casually. "We can walk back to our hotel later on."

Stan nodded and smiled and recommended The Scoreboard as having good food and reasonable prices. Underneath his parting friendliness, though, I sensed a twinge of annoyance that he wouldn't even be able to tell people where we were staying. It gave me a feeling of satisfaction to know that he'd completely failed in his quest for information.

"By the way, the last name is Reynolds," he said as we got out of the car. "I'm in the phone book. You be sure to call if you need anything. Anything at all."

Mom thanked him for everything and said she'd keep the offer in mind. She sounded so sincere that I'd have believed her if I didn't know better. There was no way she was *ever* going to call Stan.

We'd seen the last of him and his nodding head.

CHAPTER SEVEN

It was actually the next Wednesday morning before we got to move into Aunt Sarah's house. Well, it's our house now, though I suppose it will take a while before I start thinking of it that way. Mom said I could have any bedroom I wanted and I picked one of the two with a fireplace. I chose the smaller of those (which is still huge compared to most bedrooms) because it has shelves built right into the wall. There was also a big old-fashioned desk and I could picture my computer sitting on it. My bed was enormous too! Even though we were busy, I couldn't resist sprawling across it and rolling around for a minute. After years of having a narrow bed that was pretty cool.

It didn't take much time to unpack the few things we'd brought with us. Then we did some laundry, mostly the sheets and blankets from our beds, and cleaned the kitchen and our bedrooms. Right after lunch Mom took me to register for my new school.

When the form was filled out we walked up the street to Dr. Losier Middle School, which is only a few minutes away from the office where we'd registered. The principal said I could start the next morning and gave me a booklet about school rules.

We did some grocery shopping after that and then took a taxi back to the house. I unpacked the food and nearly dropped the eggs when Rosie wandered through the kitchen. It was the first time I'd actually seen her and the sight of a skunk waddling along wasn't exactly something I'd ever been used to.

She looked at me as if to say "what's your problem?" and then continued on to her dish — the only one that's not kept in the pantry. I must admit she's beautiful, though rather chubby. Maybe that's normal for skunks, I wouldn't know, but she's as round as a ball.

Rosie took her time eating and then wandered back off, probably to sleep off her food, as that seems to be her main daytime activity. I heard Stoolie tell her to mind her own business as she passed by him.

Mom and I cooked pork chops and potatoes and broccoli for dinner, which is one of my favourite meals. Once we'd eaten we did some more cleaning and then went to bed.

I had a hard time falling asleep that night. It was so strange to be in this huge house and to know it was really ours. So much had happened in the past two weeks. On top of that, I was nervous about going to a new school where I didn't know anyone. It made me think of my friends back in Ontario, which caused a big lump to grow in my throat. As I lay in bed trying not to cry, I wondered if they missed me too.

The next morning I dawdled over my breakfast until Mom got impatient and told me I was going to school and that was all there was to it. I don't know how she knew I was trying to think up some excuse to wait for another day. Moms are weird like that. It's as if they can actually read your mind sometimes.

The bell had already rung by the time I finally got there, which was when I realized my mistake in being so slow. Instead of getting to class at the same time as everyone else, I was going to have to walk in when the other kids were already at their desks.

It was all I could do not to turn around and go back home. Facing Mom would be much easier than facing a bunch of strangers. Surely I could think of some legitimate reason that I hadn't gone to class. But before I could do anything a teacher came along. She asked me who I was, took me to the office, and got the vice-principal.

The vice-principal took me to my new homeroom. As we walked down the hallway he gave me a quick lecture on the importance of getting to school on time and said he hoped I wasn't going to make a habit of being tardy. Then, as if he thought maybe he'd been too stern, he smiled and added that he was sure it wouldn't be a problem.

My homeroom teacher, Mrs. McCloskey, was a tiny woman with a squeaky voice. I cringed inwardly as she introduced me.

"Class, we have a new student," she announced perkily. "This is Sarah Gilmore. I want everyone to make Sarah feel very welcome here at Dr. Losier."

There were mumbles that could have meant anything from a few of the students. Mostly they just stared as if I were a bug under a display glass. I felt awkward in my jeans and T-shirt and wished Mom and I had been able to go shopping for some new clothes, but the lawyer hadn't finished straightening out the money yet. My outfit felt old and worn and I blushed as the other kids looked me over.

It was with relief that I took the seat Mrs. McCloskey assigned me. I opened my books and kept my eyes glued to them, trying to ignore the inquisitive looks from my new classmates. I decided that, no matter what, I was going back home at lunchtime. I'd tell Mom I felt sick to my stomach, which wasn't really a lie.

Our second-period class was in another part of the building, and as I walked along, deliberately trailing behind the others, a couple of the kids from my class joined me.

"I'm Ashley," one of them said cheerfully. "And this is Jamie."

"Hi," I mumbled, wishing they'd leave me alone.

"Where you from?"

"Ontario."

"Oh, yeah? Like, Toronto?"

"No." I couldn't help thinking that was a dumb thing to assume. Did the kids in New Brunswick think that Toronto was the only place in Ontario? "We lived in a small town near Belleville."

"Oh, yeah? Cool."

I had no idea why she thought that was cool, but I didn't say anything. I figured if I stayed quiet they'd take the hint and go away. I was wrong.

They talked all the way to the next class, mostly asking questions. Did I walk to school or take a bus? Did I have a boyfriend in Ontario? Who was my favourite music group? I gave one-word answers as much as possible, feeling more and more annoyed.

Even worse, when the noon hour came, they rushed over to me, one taking each arm.

"You can eat with us," Ashley said. I tried to protest but it was impossible to escape. They dragged me to the cafeteria, offering advice on what to buy for lunch. I fumbled in my pocket for the three dollars Mom had given me. Since I was trapped, I decided that I might as well eat before I went home. Maybe I could convince Mom that the food had upset my stomach.

I had to admit that I actually felt better after I'd had lunch. Besides, by then I'd decided that Ashley and Jamie weren't so bad after all. They were just trying to be friendly and it *was* kind of nice to have someone to sit with in the cafeteria.

Ashley told me that they were going to the mall after school on Friday and asked if I wanted to go with them.

"There's an *awesome* sale on at Suzy Shier," Jamie added. "You can use my Prestige card if you see something you want."

The thought of picking out some new outfits was tempting, even though I knew there was no money to buy anything yet. I wondered if Mom could afford to give me enough money to put a few things on layaway. Even if she couldn't, it wouldn't hurt to have a look. I said I'd ask my mother if I could go and let them know.

Then I figured I might as well stay at school for the rest of the day.

CHAPTER EIGHT

Somehow, though I'd just walked the very same route that morning, I managed to get lost on my way home that afternoon. As soon as I realized I'd taken a wrong turn I retraced my steps to the school and started over. When I finally got home the first thing I saw was a navy blue bookbag sitting on the table in the kitchen. I was leaning over it, wondering whose it was, when something rubbed against my leg, making me jump.

"Stupid cat," I muttered when I saw that it was just one of Sarah's furry friends. A laugh in the doorway drew my attention, and when I looked up I saw David coming in from the next room.

"That's Arthur the Fifth." He grinned, squatting down to pat the darned thing.

"The fifth?"

"Yep. I actually met Sarah because of this little guy."

"He's not very little," I observed as Arthur lifted his chin to be stroked. He was an enormous cat — grey with a white bandana and double paws that were also white. It looked like he was wearing a bandit-style scarf and mittens.

"Well, you didn't see him when he first got here. He was scrawny and pathetic; it was obvious that he'd been mistreated. Someone had even cut off his whiskers. My dad was on his way to work one morning and saw him being tossed out of a car on the side of the road. He brought him home but my mom is allergic to cats and we couldn't keep him."

"So you palmed him off on my mom's great-aunt."

"I guess you could say that. Everyone knew Sarah really loved animals, so Mom sent me here to see if she'd take him in. I was a bit nervous about coming over because a lot of people talked about Sarah as if she was a bit crazy." David looked alarmed then, as if what he'd said might have offended me.

"And was she?" The idea sure fit with the little I knew about Sarah.

"Crazy? No. She was different, though." He smiled. "The first thing she said when she came to the door that day was, 'Well, I see that Arthur the Fifth has arrived. I've been expecting him.' Then she invited me in."

She sounded pretty nutty to me but I kept that thought to myself as he continued.

"Sarah showed me all through the house and told me she'd been looking for someone to do some yard work and stuff. She hired me to take care of the lawn in the summer and shovel the driveway in the winter. Later, when her health started to fail, she got me to come over every day and help with the animals and other things around the place."

I felt an unexpected pang of jealousy while I was listening to him. For some reason, it bothered me to think that she was my relative but I'd never known her and he had.

"Near the end," he went on, "she told me that she was leaving the place to a great-niece who had a daughter — also named Sarah. And she asked me to give you a message."

"A message? For me?"

"Yeah. She said to tell you that you're to have her hope chest."

"What's a hope chest?"

"Some kind of old trunk, I think. I've never seen it and she didn't show me where it was. I guess it's probably out in the servants' quarters. And she made me promise that I'd tell you one more thing."

I was curious by then and leaned forward the way you do when you're about to hear a secret.

"She said to tell you this: 'Everything that matters is in the chest and I'm passing it on to you.'"

"What's that supposed to mean?"

"I don't know. But Sarah insisted that I tell you exactly that. She even got me to write it down so I'd remember."

Well, that made me even more curious and I wished I could find the hope chest right then and see what was in it. Maybe there were jewels or other valuables in there. My imagination started to come up with all sorts of interesting possibilities.

"Anyway, I have to get going now," David said, interrupting my thoughts. "Your mother asked me to stop in for a few minutes so she could write down all the pets' names and get me to show her where the electrical panel is and a few other things. I was just leaving when you got home."

"Okay, well, thanks for giving me the message and all." I watched as he gave Arthur the Fifth a final chin scratch and then sauntered out the door with a quick backward wave.

"Nice boy." Mom came into the kitchen with an armload of dishcloths and drying towels. She started sorting them into drawers, which I could see had been freshly washed too. "He really seems to have cared about my aunt."

I nodded and filled her in on what he'd told me

about the hope chest. "Can we look for it?" I asked.

"We'll have a look on the weekend," Mom answered, closing the drawers and getting out a frying pan. "I really want to get the rest of the house cleaned before tackling the servants' quarters. I had a quick look in there this afternoon and it's piled high with boxes and old furniture." She broke some eggs into a bowl and beat them with a fork. "How was school today?"

"Okay, I guess." I was disappointed that I'd have to wait to see the hope chest but didn't argue about it. Mom looked really tired. "I met a couple of girls, Ashley and Jamie. They want me to go to the mall with them after school tomorrow."

"That sounds nice. And I'm glad you've made some friends already." Mom poured some of the eggs into the frying pan and added a slice of cheese. "Wash your hands and make some toast, would you, dear? I've been busy all day, so we're just having cheese omelettes for dinner. I know it's early, but I forgot to eat lunch and I'm starved."

That was fine with me. As I stuck two slices of whole wheat bread into the toaster I couldn't help thinking how great it was to have Mom right there when I got home from school.

We'd just finished eating and were getting ready to do the dishes when there was a knock on the door. Mom went to answer it.

"Evenin', ladies. I hope I'm not interrupting anything. Just thought I'd come by and see how everything was going."

Looking across the room I saw that annoying Stan person in the doorway, smiling and nodding as usual.

Chapter Nine

I could see that Mom was as surprised as I was at Stan's appearance at our door. She told him hello and said that everything was going just fine, thank you. Then she stood there, looking a bit confused, as though she didn't quite know what to say next. She sure didn't invite him in. But did he take the hint and leave? Not Stan. He just kept smiling and nodding and remarking that he was glad to hear it and it was great that we were settled in and all.

"Big job, moving," he said once he'd run out of the other comments. "I guess the little one is in school by now, then, is she?"

Little one!

"Yes, Sarah started classes today."

"Sarah, that's right. Funny thing, that. I mean, that

there's another Sarah here now. And how do you like your new school, Sarah?"

"It's okay," I answered without enthusiasm. I wished I could think of something to say that would give him a hint that maybe he should leave — like mentioning some pressing thing Mom and I had to do.

"And what grade are you in, Sarah?"

"Seven."

"Seven, is it? Well, that's great, then."

"Uh, come to think of it, I need you to help me with some homework," I said to Mom, happy to have thought of an excuse to help her get rid of this bothersome man.

Mom grabbed at it quick. "Of course, dear," she said to me and then looked apologetically at Stan. "I'd better give Sarah a hand with her lessons. You know how it is when you change schools; there's so much to catch up on. I'm sorry I can't ask you in."

"I understand." Stan nodded some more. "Didn't mean to intrude or anything. But I was wondering…"

His voice trailed off then and he looked at the floor, his face growing red.

I'd never have guessed that Stan could ever be at a loss for words, and yet, there he was, blushing and tongue-tied. When he finally spoke again, it was in a rushed jumble that hardly made sense.

"Well, I thought, you know, where you have no car and all, it might be nice, you know, for you and the little one, uh, Sarah that is, to get out of the house for a bit. The movies I mean."

Once I realized that he was inviting us out to a movie, I felt sorry for him. Mom almost never dates, and there was *no way* she was going to go anywhere with Stan.

"The movies," Mom repeated. It looked like she didn't quite understand what he was getting at.

"For a bit of a break out of the house. The two of you." Stan's face was even redder, if that was possible. I think at that moment he wished he hadn't come over at all.

"Well, Sarah has her homework," Mom floundered.

"Yes, right." He looked perplexed for a few seconds. "Oh, I see. No, I didn't mean tonight, of course. I thought maybe tomorrow or Saturday evening. If you're not busy."

"That's very nice of you, Stan," Mom said gently. I could see she was going to let him down easy. He knew it, too; his face was all red and embarrassed.

"It's just that we have so much to do these days."

"Well, of course you do. Maybe some other time." In spite of what he said, his tone made it clear he knew there wasn't going to be another time. He looked miserable.

"But you know, I think you're right. We *could* stand to get out for a bit. A person needs to take time to relax." I couldn't believe my ears as Mom spoke up again. "We'd love to take you up on your offer, wouldn't we, Sarah?"

"Uh, sure." What else could I say?

"Well, then, that's great!" He beamed from ear to ear. And nodded. "Which night would you ladies like to go?"

"I'm going to the mall tomorrow," I said quickly.

"Saturday, then?"

The next thing I knew it was all arranged. When he'd gone I turned to Mom.

"Are you nuts? You're going out with Stan?"

"Now, Sarah, it's not really a date. After all, it will be the three of us. And you saw how terrible he felt. What else could I do?"

I could just picture it. This would only be the beginning. We'd be stuck with Stan constantly coming around with his smiling face and nodding head.

"We're never going to get rid of him," I warned.

Mom smiled at that. "I think you're making a bit much of the whole thing. It's only a movie. The poor man is just trying to make us feel welcome in a new place."

I wasn't convinced. I'd seen the way he looked at Mom, and I can't say I liked it one bit. We'd been on our own all my life and I saw no reason to complicate things by having some head-wagging guy hanging around.

On the other hand, I was probably worrying for nothing. After all, Stan wasn't Mom's type. Or, at least, I didn't think he was. To tell the truth, she hadn't really had a boyfriend for as long as I could remember. That suited me just fine. I had friends back in Ontario whose folks were split up and I'd heard lots of stories about how things went when their moms started dating.

"The guys are always nice at first," my friend Jasmine told me once, after complaining about her mom's new boyfriend. "Then they start telling you what to do. Besides, when my mom is seeing someone, she never has time for me. You're lucky that your mother doesn't date much."

Well, I can tell you one thing: If my mom starts going out with this Stan creep, he's not going to be bossing me around!

Anyway, it would be weird for my mom to have a boyfriend. The thought of her kissing some guy was enough to gross me right out. I'd never liked it when she had the odd date before, but at least they hadn't stuck around. Of course, that was when she worked six days a week. She hadn't had time for a real boyfriend then. Things were different now.

I decided right then and there that I'd have to help Mom, sort of save her from her own soft-heartedness.

I'd figure out some way to get rid of Stan.

CHAPTER TEN

School went by quickly the next day. I had lunch with Jamie and Ashley again and we talked about our plans for the mall. Ashley's dad was going to drive us and I gave them my address so he could pick me up once I'd dropped my books off at home.

Mom was in the kitchen and she jumped up the minute I came through the door.

"I went to see Nicole Standing earlier," she said, her face flushed with excitement. "She's given us an advance on the money to tide us over for now. You'll be able to shop for a few things when you go to the mall with your new friends!"

I couldn't believe my eyes when she counted out two hundred dollars and passed it over to me. I'd never had that much money to spend on clothes in a whole year, much less in one shopping trip. The coolest thing, though, was the way Mom was so happy about it.

"Be sure to get yourself a new pair of shoes, too," she added. "Remember the black ones you wanted last year, with the chunky heels? Maybe something like that."

I felt so rich I could hardly stand it.

Once I was at the mall, Ashley and Jamie showed me all the best places to shop. They seemed as excited as I was and every time I was in a dressing room trying something on, they kept running back and forth, bringing me other outfits.

I don't know how I ever would have been able to choose the clothes I finally bought without their help. There were so many nice things! But they'd look each outfit over, making me turn around and telling me if something was too tight, too loose, not right for my figure, and so on.

"That's perfect!" Ashley would squeal when something met with her approval. She'd stand me in front of a mirror. "Just look at yourself. You look great in this."

By the time we were ready to go home, I had new shoes, two pairs of jeans, a pair of black stretch pants, and four new tops. I thanked Ashley's dad for the drive and hurried into the house to show Mom my purchases.

"No, no, I want you to model everything for me," she laughed and covered her eyes when I started pulling things out of bags to show her what I'd bought. So I put on a mini fashion show, parading and turning around like models do on TV.

"They had some great sales! I even have seventeen dollars left," I said proudly when I was finished and she'd admired everything. I started to give it back but Mom shook her head.

"Keep that for spending in case you want to go somewhere with friends."

I couldn't help but think that a few weeks ago it would have been out of the question to waste seventeen dollars. Our lives had changed beyond belief, all because of a strange old woman we'd never met.

That reminded me of the hope chest.

"Please, please can we look for the hope chest now?" I begged. "I'm *so* curious. It's like torture having to wait!"

"Oh, come on then," Mom said as she hugged me. "I have to admit I'd kind of like to see what's in there too. But put something old on first. It's pretty dusty out there."

I changed in a flash and ran back down the stairs to join Mom in the servants' quarters. It was like a tiny house, except there was no kitchen anywhere. I decided that was why there were two kitchens in the main house. One must have been for the hired help.

Mom was sure right about the dust. A thick layer carpeted the floor and covered every single thing in there. That included what seemed to be a thousand boxes, old furniture, and an assortment of things like lamps and paintings standing and leaning everywhere. What a mess!

"There's more in the upstairs loft," Mom said with a sigh. "I don't know how we'll ever go through all this stuff and get the place cleaned out."

"Why bother?" I asked, thinking of all the work that would be involved. It would take forever! "It's not like we need the space."

"Well, I had an idea," Mom answered. "I thought I might be able to turn it into a business of some sort."

"You mean like a store? What kind?"

"I haven't figured that out yet," she admitted. "But it would be nice to be able to work right from home. Of course, I don't even know if I can get a licence to operate a business here. I'll have to look into zoning and things before I do anything else."

"It would be so cool to have our own business." Enthusiasm at the thought actually made me eager to help clean the place out.

"Well, don't get too excited yet. It may never come to anything. We'll have to wait and see. Now, let's find that hope chest."

We took a quick walk through both upstairs and down, looking around in case it was in plain view. No such luck. If the chest was there at all, it was hidden behind or underneath something.

"It could even be in one of the large boxes," Mom sighed. I was afraid she was going to say we'd have to leave it for now, but she didn't. Instead, she motioned me to come and help her start moving things out of the way.

"How could one person have so much stuff?" I moaned when we'd moved dozens of boxes, only to find more piled behind them. Each one had been carefully taped closed, though none of them bore labels.

"It's hard to believe, isn't it? And goodness knows what we'll find when we get around to opening them."

We lugged several others out of place, stirring up more dust to add to the growing cloud around us. I had already sneezed a few times and my eyes were starting to burn. Then we saw it.

The chest was covered by an old tablecloth but there was no mistaking the shape. We peeled the cloth off carefully, trying not to stir up too much dust, to reveal a trunk made of dark brown wood with metal strips around the sides and top.

The lid was rounded, which made it look like a treasure chest from a pirate movie. There were leather handles on either end. We each took hold of one and hauled it out to the middle of the floor.

"Let's pull it to the back kitchen and clean it up first. Then we'll see if we can get it up to your room."

It wasn't too hard to move it to the back kitchen, since we could just slide it along the floor. Once we'd washed it down, though, it was clear there was no way we were going to be able to get it up the stairs. It was way too heavy for us to carry anywhere.

"I'll see if David can stop by tomorrow evening around the time Stan is coming over," Mom said after we'd made a few unsuccessful attempts to pick it up. "I'm sure they can manage to get it to your room. In the meantime, go ahead and see what's in it."

My excitement wasn't even dampened at the reminder that we were going to a movie with Stan on Saturday evening. I kneeled down on the floor in front of the chest.

Visions of all the wonderful things that could be inside filled my head as I pulled the lid open with trembling fingers.

Chapter Eleven

It seemed that the pesky animals were as curious as I was. Arthur the Fifth and two of the other cats whose names I hadn't yet got straight came hurrying into the back kitchen as I started taking things out of the chest. Within a minute they were joined by two of the dogs. One, a terrier mix, is called Plunk because of the abrupt way he sits down, and the other one (I think) is named Dusty. Or maybe Rusty, I'm not sure.

I shooed them all away a few times and the dogs finally listened, flopping down a few feet away with their chins right on the floor and their eyes looking all sad and accusing.

The cats were another story. They kept trying to get into the trunk, mewing and making a nuisance of themselves. Instead of obeying my repeated command for them to go away, they turned impudent faces to me and rubbed against my arms so that there was soon hair floating in the air all around them. It was almost as bad as the dust out in the servants' quarters.

"Do they *have* to shed so much?"

"I suppose they do," Mom said, even though I hadn't really expected an answer to the question. "I can see that vacuuming up cat hair and cleaning out litter boxes is going to take up an awful lot of our time."

"Couldn't we give a few of them away? They're such a nuisance!"

"I'm afraid not. We've agreed to take care of them and that's what we're going to do."

"Nobody would know."

"*We* would know," Mom said quietly. I could tell that that settled it. Mom has this thing about keeping her word. Normally it's a good thing because I can always count on what she says. In this case, though, I wouldn't have minded if she broke her promise.

I gave up on trying to fight off the cats and turned back to the chest. So far, the contents were a disappointment. On top of everything else rested a lavender quilt wrapped in clear plastic, but it was the only half decent thing in there as far as I could see. Underneath it was a bunch of dishcloths and some pillowcases and doilies. I figured the good stuff was hidden in the bottom.

"I wonder why she didn't use these things," I said without much real interest in the answer. You couldn't exactly expect normal behaviour from anyone who had enough animals to fill a small zoo.

"Well, that was the whole purpose of a hope chest," Mom explained. "Years ago, young ladies made all these things by hand and put them away to be used in their homes once they were married. They never touched them until then."

"That's dumb," I commented. "You'd think your great-aunt would have eventually realized that she wasn't getting married and gone ahead and used them."

"It's strange that Sarah never married," Mom said in a faraway tone. That's the way she sounds when she's sort of talking to herself, so I didn't bother saying anything back.

"She was quite a beauty, you know."

"Old Sarah?" The idea astonished me. There were a few pictures of her around the house. I couldn't quite imagine the wizened-up old woman whose likeness looked out sternly from gold-edged frames ever being attractive.

"Oh, yes. She was lovely. I guess you wouldn't remember seeing her photographs in your grandmother's album."

A clear recollection of black and white photos came to me, pictures I'd looked at many times in my grandmother's living room. As I lifted more doilies from the chest a face rose in my mind.

"She wasn't the girl beside the tree with the big hat on, was she?"

"That was her." Mom sounded pleased that I'd remembered.

"But she…" I sneezed as cat hair floated around my nose. "That couldn't be her!"

"And why couldn't it?"

"She looked like a movie star in that picture!"

"Yes, she did. I imagine there were all sorts of young men interested in her too."

"Maybe she liked cats and dogs better, even then," I said grouchily. I was almost at the bottom of the chest by then and it was becoming clear there was nothing of any value in it. I lifted the last few items out and added them to the pile beside me on the floor. A layer of paper lined the bottom and I took it out just in case but there was nothing underneath.

"Everything that matters is in the chest and I'm passing it on to you."

Remembering Sarah's message, I felt cheated. What a weird thing to say about a quilt and a bunch of old pillowcases and stuff.

"I suppose that Aunt Sarah wanted you to have these things for the day that you're married," Mom said, as if she'd read my mind. "These are all hand-sewn and embroidered. She must have put a lot of work into them."

I wasn't cheered by the thought that her message had anything to do with me getting married and using all this junk someday. Most of it was yellowed with age anyway. But at least the chest itself was nice. It would look good in my room.

I stood up, brushing cat hair off my jeans and trying unsuccessfully to hide my disappointment.

"I'll see if I can find out what kind of detergent might take out the age stains," Mom said, as if that might perk me up. I tried to look happy at the idea, though I was secretly hoping it would all fall apart in the washer. I'd much rather use the trunk for my own stuff.

I was startled from those thoughts by a ringing sound. It was immediately followed by the sound of Stoolie saying, "Hello? Hello?"

"Oh, I almost forgot to tell you. I had a phone installed today," Mom said, as she hurried off to answer it.

I followed her down the hall and into the living room where she was lifting the receiver and saying hello. The big question in my mind was who could be calling us. After all, if she'd just had the phone put in, no one would have our number yet.

"Sarah and I were just looking through a hope chest that my aunt left to her," Mom said brightly. "No, no, it's not a bad time. We've just finished. I can chat for a bit."

I decided she'd probably called Grammie and Grampie in Ontario and given them the number. Very likely they'd phoned back when I'd be there so they could speak to me. I plunked down on the sofa waiting my turn. It would be great to talk to my grandparents.

"Excuse me for a second," Mom said. She put her hand over the mouthpiece then and turned to me. "Is there something you wanted, dear?"

"Isn't that Grammie?"

"No." She didn't look directly at me as she answered. "It's just someone for me."

Well, I knew when I wasn't wanted! I shrugged to show her I couldn't care less about her silly old phone call as I left the room. But truthfully, I *was* curious, so I listened carefully as I started slowly down the hall.

"Sorry about that, Stan," I heard her say.

Stan! The realization hit me that Mom must have phoned him first and given him our number. I quickly told myself that she'd probably only done it in case there was a change in plans for the movie tomorrow, but something in me wasn't buying that idea.

I stomped angrily up the stairs to my room.

CHAPTER TWELVE

When Mom came up to my room a bit later and asked if I wanted some ice cream I just shook my head and refused to look at her.

"How about a game of cards, then?" she suggested cheerfully, as if she couldn't see perfectly well that I wasn't too pleased with her at the moment.

"Why don't you see if *Stan* would like some ice cream or a game of cards?" I snapped. I thought I might as well make it good and clear that I wasn't happy about her talking to him.

"I think it's a bit late to invite anyone over this evening," she answered smoothly, like she didn't know I was being sarcastic.

That made me madder than ever.

"Yeah, well, I guess anyone who wanted a jerk like

him around would have to be pretty desperate for a boyfriend anyway," I muttered.

Instead of answering, she got a hurt look on her face and left, closing my door quietly behind her. I didn't feel one bit sorry for her. In fact, I was quite pleased with myself. After all, she had it coming for not getting rid of Stan right from the start. He didn't belong in our lives and the sooner she realized it and put an end to the whole thing, the better.

Right in the middle of imagining how bad she was probably feeling, my thoughts were interrupted by the sound of purring. One of the cats must have followed Mom into my room. Looking around, I found Arthur the Fifth sitting at the foot of my bed. I scooped him up, marched to the door, flung it open, and plopped him down in the hallway.

That was when I heard Mom singing. The sound of her voice rose softly from downstairs.

I couldn't believe it! She was supposed to be upset and there she was singing as if everything was just fine. I strained to listen for a moment but couldn't quite make out what the song was. It sounded happy, though. I slammed my door good and loud, crossed the room, and flung myself across the bed.

A few seconds later I felt a small thud on the bed beside me.

"I thought I just put you out," I mumbled, seeing

Arthur the Fifth's furry face staring at me curiously. The dumb thing must have sneaked back in when I was concentrating on Mom's song.

He ambled lazily across the comforter and stared at me some more. Now, this might sound stupid, but the expression on his face almost looked as though he was asking me a question.

"What do you want?" I gave him a half-hearted pat. His fur was as soft as silk. It was the first time I noticed how nice it felt. He rubbed his face on my arm, purring noisily, then flopped down against me, warm and soft and comforting.

"You can stay this once," I told him sternly, "but you don't need to think you'll be making a habit of it."

Arthur squinted in reply, yawned widely, and promptly fell asleep. He barely moved when I crawled under the covers a while later.

The next morning I was awakened by a tongue roughly washing my forehead. Sometime during the night Arthur had made his way up to my pillow and sprawled across the top of it, forming a big furry halo over my head.

"What are you doing up there?" I couldn't help laughing at the sight of his face. He looked enormously pleased with himself.

Then I remembered that I was cross at Mom. It wouldn't do for her to hear me laugh. By the time I'd showered and dressed I was in just the right frame of mind to show her she wasn't yet forgiven for calling up that Stan creep. I decided to be coldly polite toward her but when I went to the kitchen she wasn't there.

I'd kind of been counting on pancakes for breakfast since Mom always made them for me any time she was home on a weekend morning. Her pancakes are the best, big and light and fluffy. I waited for a few minutes, hoping she'd come along. Then, in case she didn't know I was up, I made some noise opening and closing cupboards and getting a glass of milk out of the fridge.

The cats and dogs were congregating around me by then, mewing and whimpering and just generally going on as if they hadn't eaten for weeks. I figured I might as well feed them. There was no sense in them being hungry too, just because Mom was apparently planning to starve me this morning.

They followed me into the pantry, and the dumb cats shoved their heads in the way as I filled the bowls. You'd think they'd know enough to stand back for two seconds until the food was in their dishes, but that would have been asking too much from this crew. I finally got the dishes all filled and went back to the kitchen. Still no sign of Mom.

I'd given up waiting and was halfway through a bowl of Cheerios when Mom showed up.

"I was really in the mood for pancakes this morning," I said accusingly. I figured she might as well know that she'd just given me yet another reason to be displeased with her.

Instead of answering right away, she went to the counter and got the coffee maker set up. It wasn't until she'd poured a cup and sat down at the table that she spoke.

"First of all, Sarah, I'm not your servant. Second, the way you spoke to me last night was inexcusable. And third, you might as well know right now that I am *not* going to put up with this attitude."

Well, that wasn't quite what I'd been expecting! Before I could form an answer, she went on.

"If I should decide to start seeing Stan, or anyone else, for that matter, I expect you to show some respect. You will *not* make snide remarks to me. You will *not* be rude, make faces, roll your eyes, or slam doors. Is that perfectly clear?"

"Yes." A lump had formed in my throat and I swallowed hard to get rid of it. Mom never talks to me that way. It made me feel horrible but I didn't want her to see that I cared. Obviously, this stupid Stan creep was more important than me.

"From the moment you were born," she went on, her voice softening, "I devoted my entire life to you. I sacrificed and struggled and did the best I could. I know you haven't had everything you might have liked, but that was never because I didn't try. And now, when things are easier for both of us, I finally have a chance to have a life for *myself*, too. I don't think that's asking too much. I've been alone for more than a dozen years and it hasn't been easy but I did it because you came first. And you still do. But there are times that life is pretty lonely for me."

Her voice trailed off in a kind of sad whisper at the end, and the sound of it cut right into me. I'd never thought of Mom as being lonely. It was a strange thing to take in. She'd never complained and I'd always thought she was perfectly content with things just the way they were. I felt selfish and mean for the way I'd acted.

"Stan seems like a nice fellow," she added slowly, as if she was being very careful about what she said. "He's kind and thoughtful, that's plain to see. Now, I don't know if he and I have much in common, or whether or not we'll ever even actually date. I admit I didn't much take to him at first, but he sort of grew on me. I've decided there's no harm in spending a little time with him and seeing where it goes. It would be nice to have someone in my life."

I told Mom I was sorry (and I really was) and promised to be nice to Stan. The weird thing was that all of a sudden I actually *wanted* her to have a boyfriend, even if it *was* someone who nodded all the time.

CHAPTER THIRTEEN

I was especially helpful to Mom all day. I thought that would make up for the mean way I'd acted last night, but even after I'd given her a hand with housework and meals I didn't feel a whole lot better. My hateful words kept echoing in my head and I couldn't stop picturing the way her face had looked when she'd left my room.

When I was dusting the living room I nearly started crying, thinking about what Mom had said to me that morning. I wondered why I hadn't ever realized that she felt lonely sometimes. I had to admit that I'd been so wrapped up in myself I'd never once stopped to wonder about her. It made me feel small and selfish.

I even volunteered for the gross, disgusting job of cleaning out the litter boxes. When we'd first moved in, I'd suggested that we pay David to keep doing that, but

Mom insisted that taking care of the cats included the unpleasant tasks. Thank goodness it only has to be done twice a week.

I swear that all these darned cats do is eat, sleep, and fill their litter boxes! My stomach churned as I emptied them into garbage bags. I rinsed them out before refilling them and sprinkled some powder that's supposed to keep the smell down. I felt so grungy when I was done that I went and took a shower, even though I'd already had one earlier. Even so, I was glad that I'd done that without complaining. It made me feel better, and the guilty feeling I'd been carrying seemed to lift a little. By dinner time, I felt almost back to normal.

We had yummy Caesar salad with chunks of chicken in it for dinner and I was just clearing the table when there was a knock on the door. I opened it, expecting to see Stan, and was surprised to find David standing there instead.

"I hear you poor helpless women need some muscle around here," he said.

I remembered then that Mom had asked him to come over so he could help Stan move my hope chest upstairs.

"Oh, yeah. Come on in."

"Hey Fester, Sammy." He squatted down to greet a couple of the cats. They rubbed against him happily. "Whatcha been up to?"

"Not much." As soon as I'd answered I realized he'd been talking to the cats, which made me feel foolish. To make it worse, I'd begun to notice that David is pretty cute. A girl hates to look dumb in front of cute guys.

"Me either," he said, smoothing over my obvious embarrassment. I was glad that at least he couldn't read my mind. He looked around as if he was searching for something to say, then came up with, "So, I guess you're all settled in and stuff."

"Yeah. Anyway, we didn't have that much with us. Just clothes, mainly."

"You like the school?"

"It's okay."

"I'm at James M. Hill this year," he said. "It's way better than the middle school. They don't treat us like babies there."

There was silence for a very long minute. Then David said it was getting warmer outside every day and I agreed that this was true. Following that remark, he added that it would soon be summer and I concurred with him on that score as well.

Thankfully another knock on the door came just then, ending our pitiful attempt to make conversation. It was Stan, nodding and smiling as usual. I reminded myself that I was going to be super nice to him.

"This is David Murray, our neighbour," I began, but my introduction trailed off when I realized I couldn't remember Stan's last name.

"David!" Stan boomed, reaching a hand out. "Nice to meet you. I'm Stan Reynolds."

"*The* Stan Reynolds?" David's eyes got bigger as Stan pumped his hand, nodding all the while. "The boxer?"

Stan got that look of someone who doesn't want to seem too pleased but can't help it. "Guilty as charged," he said, nodding some more. "You a boxing fan, son?"

"I watch some of the fights with my dad," David said excitedly. "He says you're the best amateur fighter this town's ever seen. Says you could have turned pro and had a shot at a title."

"What's this?" Mom came along then, dressed in an awesome new outfit. Her hair was a little different, too, and she had lipstick on. I blinked and stared, barely able to believe this was my mom. She looked great.

Stan stared too.

"Did I hear you say that you're a boxer?"

"A few amateur fights, hardly worth mentioning," Stan said. He had that bashful air about him that people have when they're pretending they don't want you to make a big fuss over them but they really do. He was obviously hoping Mom would be impressed.

"He's the best! Never been beaten," David volunteered with hero worship in his eyes.

"Well, I think boxing is barbaric," Mom said calmly. I stifled a giggle while Stan looked crestfallen. David's face had grown indignant, but before he could protest, Mom changed the subject.

"I asked David to come over and help move this trunk upstairs to Sarah's room," she explained to Stan, motioning toward the chest. "It's too heavy for us."

"Well, sure, no problem." Stan forced himself to sound cheerful again. "We'll get that done in jig time, won't we, David?"

They each took hold of one end and lugged it out of the kitchen and down the hall toward the stairs. Stan instructed David to go ahead up the stairs so that he would have most of the weight on him as he followed. It was comical how they both tried to act as if it wasn't that heavy for them, in spite of the fact that their faces were getting red from the effort and they were breathing in short, grunting gasps. They were winded by the time they reached the landing.

"Set it down for a minute," Stan puffed breathlessly. "We'll need to swing it around before we go on."

The second section of stairs is shorter than the first and they cleared them quickly once they'd got going again. From there, it was only a few feet to my room. I hurried in behind them as they sat the chest down with a thud.

"Well, then, Sarah, where would you like us to put it?"

I pointed to the spot I'd picked out under the window. They got it into place and then Stan pulled it forward away from the wall.

"Is it okay for me to open it?" he asked. "I need to make sure it's not too close to the wall for the lid to stay up."

I nodded. I have to admit that I thought it was nice he'd asked me first instead of just going ahead and opening it. He adjusted it a few inches at a time until there was room for the top to swing up and stay open.

"These old trunks are real works of craftsmanship," Stan said, running his hand over the surface. "I suppose you know about the compartment in the top."

"What compartment?"

"Here." He pointed to the chest's lid and then swung it open. "See how it's closed in? There should be a latch of some sort … yes, here it is." He fumbled with a metal leaf and turned it sideways. A flap fell open revealing a storage place in the rounded lid.

"Cool." David leaned forward to peer at it. "There's stuff in there, too."

My heart beat a little faster as I saw that there was indeed a number of things in there. Each small parcel was wrapped in navy blue cloth and tied with a piece of faded yellow ribbon.

I was dying to see what they held, but not with everyone standing around! And then Mom commented that we'd better get going or we'd be late for the movie.

"Say, David, why don't you join us?" Stan suggested. "My treat."

To my surprise, David didn't turn down the offer. Instead, he called home to let them know where he was going, and the next thing I knew the four of us were on our way to the theatre. I kept reminding myself that it wasn't a date or anything but I couldn't help hoping that someone from my class at school might happen to be there and see me with David.

CHAPTER FOURTEEN

I didn't know what we were going to see at the theatre until we got there. Mom had told Stan to go ahead and pick so I figured it would be a guy movie with lots of action or, if he was trying to impress Mom, a chick flick.

Instead, it was a comedy, and a pretty funny one at that. We all laughed a lot, and for a while I even stopped wondering about the other contents of my hope chest.

About halfway through the movie I noticed Stan taking hold of Mom's hand. She just kept watching the show and didn't react, but she didn't pull her hand away either. I missed an entire scene worrying that he might do something really gross like try to kiss her right there in front of me and David. Lucky for him, he didn't try a stunt like that. There's only so much a girl can stand for when it comes to her mother.

Of course, I'm not stupid. I knew that if they ended up officially dating he'd be kissing her. I just didn't want to see it.

When a few minutes had passed and he hadn't done anything disgusting, I let my attention drift back to the movie. At one really funny part David nudged my arm and nearly sent my popcorn flying. I lunged forward to save it, spilling some on a man in front of me. He turned and gave me a long, nasty look before swinging back around.

"Sorry," David whispered. Then he laughed even harder, which made me laugh too and drew yet another glare from the stranger. It seemed that he was about to say something, but Stan leaned forward.

"It was just an accident," Stan said. His tone was mild but also firm in a way that said very clearly there wasn't going to be any trouble.

When the man had once again turned back to the movie David stuck his face right next to mine, mimicking the cross scowl I'd just been given. We sank down in our seats, trying without much success to control our laughter.

I decided right then and there that we would get to be really good friends. And later on, maybe after I'd had my birthday in August and was thirteen, which is *much* older than twelve in lots of ways, we might get to be more than just friends. I still didn't know how old he was and made a mental note to ask him sometime soon, very casually of course. Then I got to wondering if he already had a girlfriend.

Another huge burst of laughter told me that I'd been daydreaming and had missed even more of the show. I munched more popcorn and made myself concentrate.

Stan offered to take us for a snack after the show and I was glad no one wanted anything. The thought of the hope chest had returned and I was anxious to get home and see what was in the neatly wrapped bundles.

We dropped David off at his house first and then pulled into our driveway. Mom asked Stan if he'd like to come in for coffee, and naturally he was only too happy to say yes. I had every intention of sitting with them, just to make sure he didn't get all mushy, but Mom gave me one of those looks that meant I was to get lost.

I started upstairs to my room but a sudden yelp made me stop and run back down to the kitchen. When I got there I found Mom doubled over laughing and Stan all red-faced. Instead of his usual nodding, he was shaking his head sideways.

"Well, now, how was I to know you had a *skunk* for a *pet*?" he said. I burst out laughing too, realizing Rosie must have wandered into the room and shocked him into letting out that funny-sounding yelp.

"Sorry," Mom kept gasping, but then she'd laugh some more. It took a few minutes for her to get herself under control and Stan's face just kept getting redder and redder.

I enjoyed the sight for a couple of minutes until Mom raised an eyebrow that made me think I'd seen all I was likely to. I went to my room then but kept the door open so I could listen. I figured as long as I could hear Mom and Stan talking, there couldn't be any smooching going on. Not that the way he'd just embarrassed himself was likely to lead to a romantic moment of any kind.

After the first disappointment over the stuff in the bottom of the chest, I was trying not to get too excited at the discovery of additional things. Still, my fingers trembled as I untied the ribbons that held together the cloth coverings of each item.

The very first package held a book. I could see right off, though, that it wasn't an ordinary book. It was bound in leather but there was no title and the pages seemed unusually thick. I opened it and read the inside flap: "Sarah Wentworth — Book One."

I flipped to the next page and quickly saw that it was a diary. I was about to toss it aside to open the rest of the things, but the first word caught my attention. I read:

January First, 1922

Tedious! A poor word to begin this journal and yet I can think of no better way to describe life here in Brockville. I am weary of days filled with nothing but those things that are designed to prepare a young woman for married life.

Evenings, I sit quietly in the parlour, embroidering cushions and listening to young men talk of their future hopes and dreams.

They are blended and become one face, these suitors. Their pronouncements of their plans are echoes of each other, recitations of the same idea. "I shall build a fine house, I shall have many acres of land, I shall provide well for my family."

I could scream. They talk endlessly of their future estates. Has not one of them a mind capable of stretching past land holdings and cattle?

Mother never fails to point out the virtues of Mr. Colby: How grand shall be his home, how lucky his bride. I know she means for me to marry him, but I cannot. He appeals no more to me than any of the other colourless men who would entice me with their dull thoughts. I dare not tell her that he has twice made me an offer of marriage. The lectures I would face if she knew I have refused him!

And the conceit of the man. He assures me most patiently that he shall not give up, that he shall win my heart. As though a woman's heart were a prize to be captured in a sporting event!

When I attempt to talk of important matters with Mr. Colby or the others, it is clear that they believe a woman's thoughts should be *centred on home and family. Even with the gains women have made, receiving the right to vote and stand for public office, we are not encouraged to speak on these things. Oh, no.*

I am continually exposed to the attitude that such things are not entirely suitable for the delicate sex. Their general opinion seems to be that our capabilities do not stretch beyond needlepoint.

Can they not see that the world is changing? Why, just last year Agnes McPhail* proved it to be so when she became the first woman elected to Federal Parliament! How I wish I could meet her and tell her what an inspiration her achievement has been to me.

But then she would be forced to wonder what she has inspired me to do! My life appears identical to that of other young women hereabouts. And yet, I know I am meant for something more. I feel it!

I yearn for a life that is different than what my situation seems to dictate. Why must the only fate deemed suitable for a young woman be that of binding herself to a man and home and children?

I long for adventure but escape from this tedium seems impossible.

It was only my burning curiosity over the other packages that made me force myself to set the diary aside after I'd finished reading the first entry.

---

* Later in 1922, Agnes McPhail changed her surname back to its original spelling, Macphail, after a visit to the family farm in Scotland.

CHAPTER FIFTEEN

Two of the other things wrapped in velvet were the same size and shape as the diary and I opened them next. Just as I suspected, they also contained Aunt Sarah's personal journals — books two and three. I sat them, along with the first, on my night table.

Now there were five other packages left. As I untied the ribbons I noticed that I wasn't as eager to find valuables as I had been before. The idea of reading about Sarah's life had captured my interest.

Three of the remaining items were boxes holding pieces of jewellery. There was a silver broach with a purple stone in it, a string of pearls, and a necklace with a creamy pink and white oval pendant that had a woman's face on it. They were pretty but I doubted that they were worth the fortune I'd dreamed about.

One package had a collection of strange things in it. There was a ring that was made out of hair, a strip of leather about two inches wide and four inches long, a scrap of silky cloth, and a paper that was rolled into a small tube and tied with string. I removed the string and carefully spread out the paper, which was stiff and crinkled. It seemed to be some kind of old ticket, though it was so faded and smudged I couldn't quite read it.

The last parcel was a wooden box containing a matching hairbrush, comb, and oval mirror with a handle. The set was beautiful, white with gold edging and tiny yellow roses painted on it, but there was a crack in the mirror.

I looked everything over for a few moments, then wrapped most of it up again and put it back into the hope chest lid. The one thing I kept out was the first diary. It would be interesting to read about Sarah's life, especially since she would have been only five or six years older than I was now when she'd started the first book.

Then, before I could even open it back up, I remembered that Stan and Mom were alone downstairs. I went over to my doorway and listened hard, but I couldn't hear any voices.

Maybe he's already gone, I thought. That's probably it. A few steps to my window on the driveway side of the house proved me wrong, though. His car was still parked there.

I paced for a few moments, pausing now and then to listen at the doorway. Nothing but silence! Images that I didn't really want to deal with kept popping into my head.

I suddenly decided I was thirsty, or hungry, or both. Any excuse to go back downstairs to see what was going on. As much as I didn't want to see any disgusting old kissing, imagining it was worse.

I tiptoed down the stairs and around the corner into the hallway leading to the kitchen. One side of the table was in clear view by then, but there was no one at it. That meant they must both be at the other side! Of course, there was only one reason for them to be sitting that close to each other. Yuck. My stomach flip-flopped nervously as I neared the room, but when I got there, I saw that it was empty.

That was when I heard their voices, trailing through the back kitchen from the servants' quarters.

"Great possibilities, all right," Stan was saying. "I can't give you a firm price right now, but I think it's safe to say you can get most of what you want done for less than three thousand dollars."

"Including new windows?" Mom asked. She sounded surprised.

"I have just what you need in my storage building." I could picture Stan's head bobbing as he spoke. "Lady out in Point Sapin just had them taken out. Wanted something fancier even though the windows she already had were like new. There are two large bay windows that will be perfect on the side, and six others, all a good size. You can decide how many you want and where they should go."

"But I can't take them for nothing," Mom protested.

"Well, I got 'em for nothin', so I'm not about to charge anyone for them. The only cost will be the labour."

"It sounds wonderful." Mom's voice was wistful. "I wish you could get started right away but it's going to take me ages to clear everything out of here."

"Well now, I'm free most evenings, Maggie. I'd be proud to come by and give you a hand with it."

The way Stan's voice sounded when he said my mom's name made me realize just how much he liked her. It was the same tone my friend Tania, in Ontario, used when she was talking about Kalan Porter. She's totally gone on him. Tania just constantly raves and raves about how much she loves Kalan, which seems kind of weird to me. After all, she's never even met him. How can you claim to love someone you don't even know?

Anyway, the way Stan said *Maggie* was a lot like that. He wasn't gushing and giggling like Tania does about Kalan, but he sure had that worshipful sound in his voice. It kind of creeped me out.

I was standing there thinking about this when the sound of footsteps told me they were coming back into the kitchen. Grabbing a glass from the cupboard, I hurried to the sink and turned on the water. When they came into the room I tried to look as innocent as I could.

"I was thirsty," I blurted before either of them had a chance to say anything, "so I was just getting a drink."

Stan smiled and nodded approvingly. "Water's the best thing there is for thirst," he said, "and it's awfully good for you too. Why, I drink about ten glasses a day myself."

"Is that right?" I tried to look as if that was the most fascinating thing I'd ever heard.

"Oh, sure. Keeps the salt flushed out of your system and helps you sweat when you're doing anything strenuous, so your pores stay nice and clear. Good for the complexion, too, though with your skin type you shouldn't have too much trouble."

He started to say something else, but Mom broke in. She told me that we were going to have to work really hard to get the servants' quarters cleaned out and that Stan was going to do the renovations to get it ready for her to start up a business. Mom isn't usually rude like that, interrupting someone who's talking. I could see that she was really excited.

"I haven't decided for sure what kind of business I'm going to open," she continued breathlessly, "but I have a few ideas. I'll make up my mind while we're getting things done. I found out there's no problem with zoning."

I promised to help as much as I could. Then I was about to go back upstairs, but Stan asked me what my hurry was.

"I was thinking we might all have a game of crazy eights," he said, nodding away.

So, to my surprise, I was included in the rest of the evening after all. We played two games of cards (which Mom won) and then ordered a pizza. After we'd eaten, Stan said he'd better be leaving. Mom and I thanked him for everything.

"My pleasure. Why, I haven't had such a nice evening since…" He hesitated, like he was deciding whether or not he should continue. Then he just said, "Well, for a long time."

I wondered why he hadn't finished what he'd been about to say.

CHAPTER SIXTEEN

Once Stan had gone and I'd said good night to Mom, I hurried to my room, eager to read more of Aunt Sarah's diary. I'd barely opened it when there was a scratching at my door.

"Go away," I said crossly. Somehow I knew it was Arthur the Fifth, though with so many animals in the house you might think that was just a lucky guess. He scratched more and mewed so pitifully that I relented and opened the door.

Arthur was there all right, but he wasn't alone. Plunk, the small dog that David had told me was part poodle and part terrier, sat beside him, his little pink tongue hanging out and his eyes as hopeful as anything I've ever seen. His whole body kind of quivered and his tail swept the floor behind him vigorously.

Arthur walked in first, looking haughty and displeased at having been forced to beg. Plunk trotted in right on his heels and jumped up on the bed as though he'd been sleeping there his whole life. And for all I knew, he had.

True to his name he plunked down, flopped his head in front of him, and closed his eyes. I wondered if that was supposed to trick me into thinking he was already asleep.

"I thought I told you that sleeping in here was a one-time deal," I reminded Arthur. "And what's the big idea, bringing a friend?"

His response was to rub against my leg and jump up onto the bed, settling beside Plunk. I put my hands on my hips and gave the pair of them the sternest look I could summon.

In reply, Arthur offered a curious glance, as if to say, "What's the big deal? Aren't you coming to bed?" Then he commenced to wash his shoulder with long noisy licks and odd sounds of satisfaction.

Plunk opened one eye, looked at me for a few seconds, and then closed it. I decided it would only be a losing battle and I was too tired to argue right then anyway.

I crawled back into bed, shoving them over a bit to make room, which didn't seem to please them much. I muttered that it was, after all, *my* bed. Plunk concentrated harder on feigning sleep but it was an obvious bit of fakery.

Arthur yawned and turned his back to me, but as soon as I picked up the diary he flopped back over, leaned up, and started licking my ear. It tickled like crazy. I told him not to be so weird. He blinked innocently and settled back down. Hoping he'd satisfied his urge to be a nuisance, at least for the time being, I opened Aunt Sarah's book and started to read.

It struck me kind of funny the way she wrote, old fashioned and formal. I guess things were pretty different back then. I gathered that they had a car but also a horse-drawn carriage, which was used by Sarah and her mother when they went anywhere. Sarah mentioned several times that she had asked her father to teach her how to drive the car, but it didn't sound as if he was going to, at least not at that point in time. It was especially unfair that Sarah's two younger brothers, Richard and Stephen, already knew how to drive. She hardly ever mentioned them, and I could see why! It was obvious that they were treated differently than she was, just because they were guys.

There were a few references to a Miss Johnson, and at first I thought she was probably a relative or something, since she was living at their house. After a while, though, I realized that Miss Johnson was a servant.

There were also two men who lived in what Sarah called the west wing of the house. They seemed to be hired hands. She called them Berkley and Patterson, which I took to be their last names. Berkley always drove the carriage when Sarah and her mom went anywhere.

I found it odd that she called the female servant Miss Johnson, while she didn't use Mr. with the men's names. Then I came to a passage where she mentioned that Miss Johnson's family had fallen on hard times, which made it necessary for her to accept a position below her station in life.

Sarah wrote: "One can only admire Miss Johnson's pleasant deportment in the face of such misfortune. To be raised as a gentlewoman and be thus lowered must be a bitter tonic to swallow. I wonder if I could manage as well as she, should I be reduced to similar circumstances."

A lot of what she wrote about was just ordinary stuff, but it sounded different the way she said things. I wondered what it would be like to talk that way, all stiff and formal. I couldn't help giggling, imagining myself meeting David and saying something like, "How do you do, Mr. Murray?"

Plunk shifted then, squinted, stretched his front legs, and shoved them against my shoulder, as if protesting that I was taking up too much space. I rearranged him and gave him a pat to soothe him back to sleep. Then I continued reading.

A lot of what Aunt Sarah talked about was how she didn't like Brockville and how much she longed to get away. I felt sorry for her, even though it had all happened years ago. It did sound as if her life was pretty boring. Besides that, there were no guys around that interested her.

Then, I came to this passage!

March 30

A stranger arrived in Brockville last week, causing a flurry of speculation among the townsfolk. It wasn't long before word of his affairs had spread through the whole town.

The gentleman is Mr. Anderson King, a wealthy business-man from the east coast. It seems that he has come to build a factory for the production of an improvement for the modern auto-mobile, although I've not yet heard the exact details.

Today, Mother and I were in town picking out dry goods for our summer frocks when Mr. King came into Hamilton's General Store to set up an account. He introduced himself to Mr. Hamilton, and I noted, as the two gentlemen shook hands, that Mr. King's were well manicured and without that rough look so common to the local working class.

He bowed gracefully to Mother and me and it seemed that his eyes rested on me for several seconds longer than was necessary. I flattered myself that he was not displeased with what he saw.

I must say he's the most handsome man I've ever seen. He was dressed in a fine woollen day suit of deep grey, and the cut of his garment left no doubt that it had been expertly tailored. His shoes were black leather and had recently known the attention of polish, unlike the all-too-often scuffed and muddied shoes of Brockville men.

I must confess that I tarried over my selections in the hope that Mr. Hamilton would make introductions, but this did not happen. Mr. Hamilton was too busy fawning over his important visitor, no doubt pondering the large amount of business Mr. King would bring to him. This lack of manners shamed me, and I wished I could implore Mr. King not to make assumptions thereby on the general refinement of the townsfolk.

When Mother and I had finished our business, she made a point of talking of the merits of Mr. Colby on our journey home. All the while, my thoughts were wholly taken with Mr. King.

I wonder if I shall ever have the pleasure of being presented to him.

I was wondering the same thing! It all sounded so romantic, the handsome stranger in town. I longed to know whether or not Aunt Sarah ever got to meet Mr. King, but my eyes were getting heavier and heavier and the words kept blurring.

With some reluctance, I laid the diary aside, turned off the light, and fell asleep to the sound of Arthur snoring softly beside me.

Chapter Seventeen

We were up earlier than usual on Sunday morning, although for different reasons. Mom was spurred into action by her eagerness to get started on the servants' quarters, while I was wakened by Arthur the Fifth's scratchy wet tongue on my nose. I gave him a lecture on proper morning manners but I don't think he got it. In any case, all he did was yawn and blink questioningly.

"You are *not* sleeping in my room any more if you're going to pull stunts like that," I threatened. His response was to stretch and jump down off the bed. I tried to convince myself that was a sign of comprehension and repentance, but deep in my heart I knew he just wanted his breakfast.

Plunk was up like a flash the second my feet touched the floor, and it was obvious what he wanted. I hurried to the bathroom and then hauled on some clothes to take him and the other dogs out for their morning walk — always a matter of some urgency with them.

There were pancakes cooking when I got back and breezed into the kitchen. I filled the dishes for the furry crowd and then washed my hands in the kitchen sink and sat down to wait for my pancake. It occurred to me that kids are a bit like pets, waiting anxiously for their food to be served.

Mom was humming and smiling as she moved about the kitchen and I suspected her mood was because of Stan. For a second, that kind of upset me, but then I reminded myself that I'd decided to be mature and reasonable about the idea of Mom having a boyfriend.

"I think I've made up my mind on what kind of business I want to start," she announced while we were eating. "Crafts! They're always popular and I've heard that a lot of local people make beautiful things. Many of them sell their products at events that are set up here and there. That means they have to store everything in between sales events, rent tables, and so on. I was thinking that if they had somewhere that they could display their work year round, they'd probably be glad to do it. So, I'm going to open a craft store."

"How would you make money for yourself if you're just selling other people's stuff?" I asked, chasing a bite of pancake with a cold drink of milk.

"I'd charge a monthly fee for tables, probably not much more than they'd pay to rent one for a weekend somewhere else. And I'd earn a commission on sales. On top of that, I'd have a section where I'd carry a lot of the supplies they need to make their things. Without any overhead, I could probably offer them supplies at a better price than they pay other places."

"It sounds pretty good."

"I think it will work out well. Another thing, it won't cost me anything to decorate because some of the crafts will be displayed on the walls." She got up, scraped half of her pancake into the garbage, and poured coffee. "Any ideas on what we might call it?"

We talked about possible names for the business for a while but none of them seemed quite right. By then, we'd finished eating and doing the dishes.

"Well, I guess we'd better get at it," I said. I knew my enthusiasm probably wouldn't last too long once we started going through all the boxes. "The only thing we've cleared out of there so far is the hope chest."

"That's it! That's the perfect name!"

"What?"

"The Hope Chest. That's what we'll call the store."

Well, I felt anything but hopeful once we got out there. It seemed impossible that we'd *ever* finish sorting through the piles of boxes and furniture. There was also the question of what we were going to do with it all.

"Some of this stuff, like old clothes, can go straight out to the garbage." Mom sighed, looking around her. "And Stan suggested that we could hold a yard sale to get rid of lot of things."

We'd gone through seven dusty boxes and filled a couple of garbage bags with things no one in their right mind would ever want, when we heard Stan's voice.

"Hello? Hello? Anybody home?"

"We're out here," Mom yelled back. She straightened up from the box she'd been bent over and turned to face him as he came through the doorway.

"Morning, ladies." Stan's face appeared around the corner. "I thought I'd find you hard at work. Came by to give you a hand, if that's all right."

It was sure all right with me!

"Uh, wait, I think I might have the wrong place." He peered at us closely one at a time. "I'm looking for the Gilmores."

Then he leaned toward Mom. "Maggie! It *is* you. I thought I'd wandered into a hobo's house!"

I was laughing at that until he added, "And I suppose this unusually large dust bunny is your lovely daughter, Sarah."

It was true that we weren't exactly clean. Both of our faces were dirty and smudged, but Mom assured Stan that he'd look the same in no time.

"Might be an idea to open these windows and let

some air in," Stan suggested. "Help clear some of the dust out."

The windows were old wooden-framed things that seemed as though they hadn't been opened in years. It took quite a bit of persuasion before Stan could get them open, but once he did, a fresh breeze soon improved the stale smell and the dust started to clear a little.

Before long, we'd fallen into a routine. Mom and I tossed things that were to be thrown out into a growing pile, which Stan started to bag once he'd made some progress with arranging things. In another section we stacked all the stuff that was good enough to sell. There were also a few things we decided to keep.

By noon we'd made more progress than we could have thought possible, and things were starting to look a bit more hopeful. Mom, on the other hand, looked downright ridiculous. She had grey streaks through her hair and splotches of dirt on her face, with a big one right in the middle of her nose. She reminded me of a bag lady, the kind you see on television sometimes. I figured I didn't look much better.

"I'm getting kind of hungry," I said when one o'clock had come and there'd been no mention of lunch.

"Goodness, will you look at the time!" Mom's hands brushed her face again, wiping hair away and depositing even more dust. "I'll make some soup and sandwiches."

"No need for that," Stan said quickly. "I brought along a little something. Took the liberty of putting it in the fridge. Hope that was all right."

The "little something" looked more like a feast to me. There was a tray of cold cuts with cheese and pickles, sliced tomatoes and cucumbers, potato salad, fresh bakery rolls, and a white cake with chocolate frosting. We cleaned up, set the table, and dug in.

I ate too much, which made me feel lazy afterward. The last thing I wanted to do was go back out and sort through more of Aunt Sarah's junk.

And then, miraculously, I was saved by the phone. It seemed like an extraordinary bit of good luck — at the time.

CHAPTER EIGHTEEN

"**I**s this Sarah?" The voice coming through the phone line seemed breathless, as though the caller had just run up and down a flight of stairs.

"Hello? Hello?" screeched Stoolie behind me. "Who's calling please? Hello?"

"Yeah," I said. "Who's this?"

"Jamie."

I paused, then said, "Oh, hi."

"Don't sound so excited!" she laughed.

"Sorry," I said, "you just caught me off guard. I didn't think you had my phone number."

"I didn't. But Directory Assistance did. Anyway, a bunch of us are going to the pool. Wanna come?"

"I don't think I can," I said glumly. The thought of a nice cool swim was sure appealing after spending the morning in a hot, dusty room. "I'm supposed to be helping my mom."

"Well, *ask* your mom anyway. Look sad and tell her everyone else is going. That always works for me."

"I'll ask," I promised, knowing I'd never pull off that kind of performance. Mom would see right through it and she'd never let me go then.

"Okay, do your best. You know where the pool is?"

"Yeah. I pass it on the way to school."

"Oh, you mean the one by the old rec centre. That one's not open yet. This is an indoor pool." She gave me quick directions. "Meet us there at three if you can get away."

"I'll try." I hung up the phone without much hope that Mom would let me go.

When I went back to the kitchen, Mom and Stan were cleaning up from lunch. I told her about the invitation and waited for her to remind me that we had a lot of work ahead.

"A swim sounds grand," Stan spoke up before she could say anything. "And isn't that great, how she's made some friends already, Maggie? Must make it a lot easier, being in a new place and all."

Well, after that it would have been pretty near impossible for Mom to say no. She hesitated only a second before telling me to go ahead.

"And have fun!" Stan added. Of course he was nodding vigorously as he spoke, but it didn't seem quite so annoying this time.

I could hardly believe my good fortune. Escaping from the drudgery to go swimming! I dashed up the stairs to get ready, but as I reached my room I remembered something. The bathing suit I had was last year's, and it was faded and kind of tight. To be perfectly honest, it hadn't been what you could call stunning when it was new. Now it looked like something you'd mop the floor with. It just plain wasn't fit to wear.

I swallowed hard, trying to think of what to do. There was no way I was going to be seen in that suit, especially with a bunch of kids I hardly knew. I slowly made my way back to the kitchen.

"Uh, I've decided to stay home and help after all," I said, trying to look as if sorting through dusty boxes suddenly appealed to me much more than swimming. Mom and Stan looked at me in astonishment.

"That's awfully responsible of you," Stan praised me with more hearty head bobbing. "But a girl your age should be out having a good time with her friends. We can manage just fine without you."

Mom's reaction was a little different. She looked at me with narrowed eyes and her mouth went into a hard line. "What's going on, Sarah?" she asked with a hint of anger in her voice. I couldn't understand it.

"Nothing."

Without another word, Mom took hold of the back of my elbow and led me down the hall and around the corner. Then she whirled around to face me. "I know exactly what you're up to."

I stared at her in confusion while Stoolie told us to knock it off.

"You don't want to go because that would leave Stan and me alone here," she accused hotly.

"That's not true," I protested, feeling tears forming in my eyes. Anger swelled up in me at the accusation, especially after I'd been so careful to be nice to Stan.

"Oh, isn't it? Then why the sudden change of heart?"

"My bathing suit is gross, that's why. I can't go swimming without something decent to wear."

Mom got this odd look on her face — kind of a mixture of embarrassment and horror — as she realized how unfair she'd been. Within seconds, her expression crumbled and I thought she was about to cry.

"Oh, Sarah, honey, I'm so sorry." She reached out and pulled me into her arms. After a long hug, during which she seemed to compose herself, she told me to wait there for a minute. She hurried back to the kitchen, where I could hear a hushed conversation taking place. Then she came and got me.

"We'll take you to get a new suit right now," Mom told me, smiling. "Come on, you still have time to meet your friends at the pool."

The three of us piled into Stan's car, and five minutes later we were at the mall. I found a bathing suit quickly. It was one piece, black with a wide, yellow, V-shaped section going down the centre of the front. Mom didn't even say anything about the price, which was more than we'd ever spent for something like that. She just nodded and told me to go try it on.

Stan had disappeared while I was in the fitting room, and when he came back he had a big shopping bag with him.

"She'll need a bathing cap, too," he told Mom. "Pool regulations."

We found a black cap, paid for the two items, and headed back. As soon as we got home I ran up the stairs to change. I discovered what Stan had bought when I came back downstairs.

"Uh, Sarah, this is for you," he said, looking kind of shy and embarrassed. As he spoke, he pulled a huge, fluffy beach towel from the bag and passed it to me. It was brilliant blue with bright yellow ducks on it — a mother and four babies.

"It's beautiful. Thank you so much." My throat was tight all of a sudden, and the words came out kind of funny and flat. I hoped Stan didn't think it was because I was forcing myself to say thank you, the way you do when you get a boring present, like flannel pyjamas or something.

"Aw, it's nothing. You just have a good time."

He drove me to the pool then, which was probably a fifteen- or twenty-minute walk from our house. When we got there he made me recite the route I'd need to take to get back home.

As I walked into the big building that housed the pool, a gym, and a rec centre, I couldn't help but admit that Stan was a really nice guy. There he was, spending his Sunday helping us when he probably had a lot of better things to do. He'd brought lunch, too, which was really thoughtful. But it was the towel that clinched it. I don't think my view of him was improving because he'd bought me a towel. I think it was because he'd *thought of it* in the first place.

That makes what happened next a whole lot worse.

CHAPTER NINETEEN

There was already a bunch of kids in the pool and I stood there for a moment trying to locate Jamie among the swimmers. By the time I saw her, with Ashley and a couple of other girls, on the far side of the pool, she'd noticed me too.

"Come on in," she hollered and waved.

I stepped up to the side, but before I could jump in the lifeguard on duty hurried over to me.

"You can't go in without a bathing cap."

Darn! I'd had the bathing cap with the towel I was planning to bring before Stan gave me the new one. I must have left it at home when I tossed the old towel on the kitchen table. Swimming would be half over by the time I went back for it but there was no choice.

"I forgot my cap at home," I yelled to Jamie. "I'll have to go back and get it."

"What?"

"I said I have to go home," I yelled louder, realizing that with her bathing cap on she couldn't hear me over the noise of the other swimmers.

She shook her head to let me know she still couldn't hear me, then swam to the end of the pool and climbed out. A couple of the other girls, including Ashley, came along with her.

I started to explain, but before I got very far, one of the girls interrupted to point out that the tag was still on my bathing suit. Jamie giggled and yanked it free while I blushed.

"I had to go to the mall for a new suit," I said, trying to join the laughter, "and I was in such a hurry I must have forgotten to take it off."

"I thought your mom didn't have a car."

"She doesn't. Stan, uh, a friend of hers, was at our place and drove us over."

"Oooooh. A *boyfriend*."

"That must be the guy I saw with you and your mom at the show," piped up a girl I didn't even know.

"Wow, your mom sure works *fast*. You guys just got here."

"He's *not* her boyfriend," I protested to the clamour of voices and giggles.

"Oh, *sure* he's not."

"He's *not*!" I insisted angrily. They were acting like my mom was trashy or something. My denial was met with rolled eyes and more snide remarks. One of them made slurpy kissing sounds. I felt like hitting her.

"I'll have you know that my mom wouldn't go out with Stan if he was the last guy on earth," I yelled angrily. "He's like, a total geek. My mom has better taste than that."

For a few seconds I thought I'd shut them up. The laughter stopped suddenly and there were no more comments. Then I became aware that a few of them were darting uncomfortable glances behind me.

I turned to see what they were looking at, and there, to my horror, stood Stan, holding my bathing cap in his hand.

"I ... thought you'd be needing this, Sarah," he said. His voice was missing its usual booming exuberance. "You forgot it in the kitchen."

I could see by the look on his face that he'd heard what I'd just said. This awful feeling hit me hard in the stomach, like the kind you get when you've just been caught doing something really horrible and you know there's not the slightest chance you can worm your way out of it.

I wished I could take back the mean remark, but it was too late. Stan's eyes were really hurt but he forced a smile as he passed me the cap.

"Enjoy your swim," he said quietly. Then he turned and left, while I stood there holding the cap and feeling wretched.

The worst thing was that I hadn't meant what I'd said at all. Stan had been nothing but kind and helpful to us since we first got here, and I knew perfectly well that my mom was starting to like him a lot. I couldn't figure out why I'd made the cruel comment that he'd heard. It had just come out.

Swimming was the last thing on my mind at that point, but the only other option was going home and facing Stan and Mom. That was out of the question! I wondered what I was in for later and what Mom would have to say about the whole thing. It wasn't going to be good, but then I knew that I deserved whatever I got.

The whole time I was in the pool, all I could think about was Stan's hurt face and what Mom's reaction was going to be. I had the worst possible time ever. The two hours went by unbelievably slowly as I tortured myself with thoughts of what I'd done, but then, oddly enough, when it was over, the time seemed to have flown by.

I dried myself off on the towel Stan had bought, feeling even worse, and made my way home in a state of pure dread.

As I rounded the corner to the house, I could see that Stan's car was no longer in the driveway. At least I didn't have to face him right away.

Mom was in the kitchen, setting the table for us to eat. She'd laid out leftovers from the great lunch Stan had brought — another reminder to add to my guilt.

"Hi, sweetie," she said cheerfully when she saw me. "I imagine you're hungry as a bear after your big swim. Did you have a good time?"

I knew immediately that he hadn't told her! It hadn't even occurred to me that he might not, and I could hardly believe my good fortune.

"Sarah? Is something wrong?"

"No," I said quickly, "I'm just tired." It was true, too. The enormous relief left me with a sudden exhausted feeling, as though my whole self had sagged inward.

"Tired! At your age!" She laughed. "Well, come and eat. That might help your failing strength pick back up."

The food that had been so delicious at lunchtime tasted like sawdust to me then, but I forced enough down to keep Mom from getting suspicious. Afterward, I did the dishes and mopped the kitchen floor. Both tasks were finished by six o'clock and the whole evening stretched out before me with nothing to occupy me but my guilt.

Mom said she couldn't face doing any more work in the servants' quarters that night and asked if I'd like to get a movie. I told her I didn't really feel like it, not wanting to be around her at the moment, as if avoiding her would help me forget what I'd done.

Instead, I went to my room and tried to concentrate on Aunt Sarah's diary. To my surprise, it worked.

April 12

What a wonderful day this turned out to be, in spite of early indications to the contrary. The twins, Eliza and Burgess Fennel, had invited me to a card party, an event I normally detest. Not that I mind playing hearts, which in itself is a pleasant enough pastime. No indeed, but what passes for wit in the accompanying conversation wears thin very quickly.

Mother insisted that I must go, though I tried to beg a sick headache. I might have managed the excuse if I'd thought of it earlier in the day, but alas, it was nearly time to leave when Mother reminded me of the event.

"You spend too much time in solitude," she said brusquely, "and not enough with people of your own age. Now, get dressed. Your father is sending the carriage around directly."

It was useless to protest. I put on my brown dress with the gold collar and went with some reluctance.

The other parties had already arrived and I waited in the hallway for what seemed ages before Eliza came to take me to the others.

"Mr. Anderson King is here," she whispered as we walked toward the parlour, where tables had been arranged for the games. The very mention of his name made my heart quicken, though I

said nothing. How I wished I'd worn my blue dress, which is ever so much nicer than the brown!

I felt certain that I was flushed when we entered the room and I could only hope that no one would guess the cause of my heightened colour.

"Allow me to present my dear friend, Miss Sarah Wentworth." Eliza's voice was full of importance as she introduced me to Mr. King. Of course, he was most proper, bowing and declaring himself delighted to make my acquaintance. I felt at once that these words carried meaning beyond their formality, an impression that grew steadily throughout the evening.

Unlike the local ruffians, Mr. King was attired in a proper evening suit. I must say that this served to enhance his attractiveness, although he would be handsome in farmer's wear.

During the third game, at which time I was seated in that gentleman's company, Mr. King solicited my opinion on several matters of discussion. In fact, so steady were his attentions to me that I felt sure he would inquire as to when I might be receiving visitors. The one disappointment in the whole evening was that he made no suggestion of calling on me. Still, all in all, it was a glorious night, and one that shall not soon be equalled.

I confess that, for the first time in my life, thoughts of courtship and romance are not so unappealing after all.

CHAPTER TWENTY

I fell asleep reading Aunt Sarah's diary and woke in the morning to find my light still on and Arthur the Fifth purring contentedly on the pillow beside me. I vaguely remembered Plunk being there through the night too, but he was nowhere to be seen when I got up.

The clock told me it was past nine, and for a moment I thought I was going to be late for school. Then I remembered that it was Victoria Day and we had the day off. But it was pretty late, and I was supposed to help Mom with the servants' quarters again, so I scrambled out of bed and hurried to wash and get dressed. Then I headed to the kitchen.

I could hear from the shuffling sounds that Mom was already hard at work. A peek out the window to see if Stan was there too told me the coast was clear for the moment. At least, there was no sign of his car.

I had a glass of orange juice but didn't bother with breakfast. To be perfectly honest, I had no appetite at all. The thought of facing Stan if he happened to come over made my stomach churn with guilt and embarrassment.

Arthur's appetite, on the other hand, was just fine, as he quickly let me know with loud, demanding meows. I poured some food into his dish and was amused to see a couple of other cats come running at the sound, even though I knew they'd already been fed. Filling a few other bowls to make sure none of them tried to bully Arthur, I made my way out to join Mom.

"Morning, dear." She smiled. "You must have been worn out from all the work and swimming yesterday. I saw neither hide nor hair of you after you went upstairs."

"I guess I was pretty tired," I agreed. "What time did you get up?"

"Six," she said cheerily. "I wanted to get a good head start on things so when Stan gets here he won't think I'm taking advantage and leaving things for him."

"What time is he coming?" I asked, hoping she couldn't hear the dread in my voice.

"I'm not sure, but he told me yesterday morning that he'd be around to help all weekend, so he'll probably come walking in any time."

He didn't arrive during the morning, though. We worked steadily and Mom tried not to keep looking at her watch, but once in a while I saw her glance down at it. By noon she'd gotten a little quieter and less cheerful.

"Something must have come up," she said as she opened a can of soup for our lunch. "I'm sure Stan told me he'd be around today. Or maybe I misunderstood him."

By then I knew that Stan wasn't coming, but I couldn't tell her that. What was I supposed to say, "Actually, Mom, I insulted Stan pretty bad at the pool yesterday, so I don't imagine we'll be seeing any more of him"?

The afternoon went by slowly, with Mom stopping to listen every time she heard a noise outside. Her face would get hopeful for a few seconds and then fall with disappointment, which she tried to hide from me. I had to pretend that I didn't notice anything was wrong, which wasn't easy since I felt like crying the whole time. I'd ruined everything.

We called it a day around five, ate, and did the dishes. As we were finishing up, the phone rang and Mom hurried to answer it. I knew she was hoping it would be Stan, but it was David, calling to ask if we wanted our lawn mowed after school the next day.

I suggested a game of crib. We hadn't played since we got to New Brunswick, mostly because there were so many other things to do. I figured it might distract Mom from worrying about why Stan hadn't showed up or called. She said okay, but after half-heartedly shuffling the deck for a few minutes, she admitted she really didn't much feel like playing.

"I think I'll catch up on my correspondence." Her voice was kind of sad and worried, though I could see she was trying to sound normal. "I haven't written to anyone since we got here."

Feeling terrible, I went up to my room and picked up the diary. It seemed to be the only thing that took my mind off what I'd done. It's amazing how cool it was to read about Aunt Sarah's life, stuff she'd written when she was still a teenager with her whole life ahead.

It was like a novel, only it was true. What a strange thing to think that the young girl in the diary was the same person as the old lady who'd just died.

April 20

There is much excitement in the air today. Last evening, Mr. King held a meeting at the town hall, where he presented his business proposition. After weeks of speculation and gossip, we are finally aware of his reason for being in Brockville.

Most of the local men attended and Father was no exception. I tried very hard not to appear too eager to hear of it at the breakfast table this morning, though anything related to Mr. King has become most interesting to me.

"He's a mighty convincing fellow," Father declared, as he told Mother and me about the evening. "A lot of the men signed up on the spot after seeing his sketches and business plan."

"What sort of business is it?" I asked, taking care to keep my voice casual.

"Production of a new automobile." Father shook his head then. "I must say that it looks good on paper. This King fellow says he's putting half the money into the business and raising the other half from locals. Claims he doesn't believe in doing it any other way, because if the locals are involved, and stand to make a lot of money, everything goes a lot smoother than if there's just an outside investor creating jobs and realizing all of the profits. And of course, putting up half the money himself proves his own commitment, so to speak. Went on about teamwork a good deal."

"That makes sense," Mother said mildly.

"I suppose it does. It's the figures that I wonder about. According to Mr. King, investors will see a return of ten times their initial outlay inside of five years, and as much as fifty times in ten. That would turn three hundred dollars into fifteen thousand in ten years."

"My goodness," Mother said.

"Sounds too good to be true," Father said. "And from my

experience, if something sounds too good to be true, it probably is. I don't like to be sceptical, but that's how I feel."

This angered me. Mr. King is obviously a great visionary. It's men like Father who hold this town back from a real chance of growth and success. I wasn't the least suprised when Father said that the whole thing was too speculative and he had no plans to invest.

How I wish I was entitled to the inheritance set aside for me on my grandfather's death, but that won't be mine until I'm twenty-one. Of course, it's expected that I will be married at that time, and my property will become my husband's. I would invest my money and be wealthy and independent in a few years, if only I could.

Sometimes it's just horrid being a woman!

So! Aunt Sarah had an inheritance too! Only, she was held back from doing what she wanted with it. Her gift to us suddenly meant even more to me.

Chapter Twenty-One

My mind was anywhere but on my work at school on Tuesday, which wasn't going to help when we had a test in English on Thursday. I barely paid attention to the story we were reading and instead kept drifting off to thoughts of Stan and what was going to happen with him and whether or not Aunt Sarah ever got to know Mr. King better.

It occurred to me that maybe Stan would come around while I was at school. Mom hadn't looked very happy at breakfast, and it was awful to think I'd caused that, even though she didn't know it.

Ashley and Jamie were getting together at Jamie's place after supper, and they asked if I wanted to come too.

"No," I said, without giving an explanation. For some strange reason, I felt angry at Jamie, as if it was *her* fault that I'd said those mean things about Stan. It was like I blamed her because she'd asked me to go swimming, since nothing bad would have happened if I hadn't been there. I guess that was stupid, but that's how I felt.

It wasn't the smartest thing to do, putting off the only two friends I'd made since we got here. After all, school would soon be out for the summer and it was going to be pretty long and boring if I didn't have anyone to hang around with. None of that seemed to matter very much at that moment, though.

Mom was peeling potatoes when I got home, and I could smell chicken cooking in the oven. One glance at her told me that Stan hadn't been around as I'd hoped he would.

"Hello, dear." She smiled without much behind it. "How was your day?"

"Good. Yours?"

"Busy. I did a lot more out there." She inclined her head toward the servants' quarters. "I think it will be cleared out by the end of the week. I'm going to put an ad in the paper for a yard sale this Saturday to try to sell off some of the stuff."

That was when I remembered that Stan was supposed to do the renovations. I mentioned that to Mom, real casual like, but it didn't seem to cheer her.

"Well, yes, I did talk to him about that. We'll see.

There are other contractors around, so I'll probably get quotes from a few others too."

I could see from the way she'd answered that she wasn't going to contact Stan about doing the work if she didn't hear from him first. Mom has too much pride to call him — not when she had the impression he didn't want anything to do with her anymore.

I knew she had to be wondering what happened, why all of a sudden he'd just stopped coming around or phoning. She probably thought he'd lost interest in her. I wished I could get up the nerve to tell her the truth, but even the thought of explaining it made me feel sick.

A couple of times I tried to force something out, but no words came. It was as if my mouth was frozen or the words were stuck partway out or something.

We ate dinner, though neither of us could get much down. I snuck a few bites to Plunk, who seemed to be around me constantly these days.

Arthur the Fifth, too. I've almost stepped on him half a dozen times. The other cats were pretty aloof, just hanging around the house and only bothering with us when they wanted something to eat. Not Arthur. He made a regular nuisance of himself!

I did my homework after we were done eating and cleaning up. While I was trying to concentrate on the story we'd started in English that day, a buzzing sound started up outside, startling me into dropping my book.

Looking out my window, I saw that it was David mowing the lawn.

Almost as if he had built-in radar, he glanced up at the window, saw me there, and waved. I felt like an idiot, with my nose squashed against the pane, looking down at him like some kind of reverse Peeping Tom. If that hadn't happened, I could have taken him a glass of water later and maybe had a chat. He might even have been able to give me some advice on the problem I'd created with Stan. After being caught looking out the window, though, there was no way I was going outside to talk to him.

Instead, I finished reading my story, did my other homework, and got out the diary. I'd nearly reached the end of the first one, and I was wondering if Aunt Sarah ever got to know Mr. King any better. The very last entry gave me my answer.

May 04

He has come! Mr. King has come to call on me. It matters not that Mr. Colby was there already, seated in his usual chair by the mantle, attempting once again to engage me in the tedious talk of his grand future — in which it appears he still supposes I shall have a role. At least Mother is of some use at such times, happily agreeing with his every word and throwing me meaningful glances meant to encourage my participation. I find it quite easy instead to pretend fascination with my needlework and to answer her efforts to draw me into the conversation with polite, single-word replies.

As we were being thus entertained, Miss Johnson arrived in the doorway and announced Mr. King. He strode into the room looking remarkably fresh for one who has been so busy with important business matters.

Mr. Colby made an attempt at amiability, but a good deal of his posturing was transparent indeed. It was apparent that he felt his position as my number one suitor was threatened, and how could it not be? A man such as Mr. King, a wealthy, successful man of the world, makes the locals look even commoner.

I found my needlework much less intriguing from that point forward and conversed with Mr. King on a variety of matters. He is so well informed on every subject and was most keen to hear my views on politics, social issues, and even business. It was refreshing to have an audience for thoughts I have previously kept to myself.

Mr. Colby insisted on interjecting ideas and opinions. Mr. King listened politely before challenging them with wit and ease. I felt almost sorry for Mr. Colby as he made himself look more and more ridiculous and unlearned. His disgruntlement grew until at last he took his leave, though not before promising pointedly to call again on the morrow.

It was then that Mr. King suggested a refreshing turn about the property. He and I strolled through the apple orchard and up the slope until we reached the river. From there, we proceeded along its banks and spent an enjoyable half-hour talking as easily as old friends before returning to the house.

My one fear is that I, along with the entire community, must appear hopelessly behind the times and unsophisticated to a man such as Mr. King.

Although I cannot help but believe that his interest in me goes beyond friendship, he did not speak of a second visit, nor issue an invitation to my family to attend at the home he is letting from the Butlers.

CHAPTER TWENTY-TWO

My interest in Great-Aunt Sarah was getting stronger and stronger. From the last entry I'd read, it seemed that she and Mr. King might be falling in love with each other. It was exciting. On the other hand, I knew she never married. Something must have gone wrong between them.

When we'd first come to live in Miramichi, I'd only seen her as a kind of batty old woman with a house full of animals. Now I found myself wishing that her life had turned out differently, as though wanting it could make it so. It was obvious that she could have married (if not Mr. King, then someone else) and had a family, but she hadn't. Why had she ended up alone in a rambling house?

That thought jumped to others and ended up reminding me that I hadn't been what you could call nice to Ashley and Jamie the last time I'd talked to them. If I didn't watch it, I was going to end up as alone as my great-aunt.

Or my mom. My insides felt all weird every time I thought about how I'd busted things up between her and Stan. I have to admit that the sickish feeling I got was partly because I was sorry for what I'd done and partly because I was worried she was somehow going to find out. But then, it didn't look like Stan was going to call her again, so maybe she never would.

There was also a lot of guilt, not only because she'd told me about being lonely, but also because I'd wanted to get rid of him at the beginning.

I tossed and turned for a long time before I fell asleep with the usual pair of intruders beside me on the bed.

Plunk was at the door pawing to get out of the bedroom and going on something terrible the next morning, which woke me up. I mumbled for him to knock it off a couple of times and then got up when it was clear that he had no intention of stopping. My bedside clock told me it was barely after six.

"What's the big idea?" I asked him crossly. "I could have slept for another hour."

He kind of bounced in one spot, wagging his tail furiously and giving a little "ruff."

"You're nothing but trouble," I grumbled. He

jumped up against the door again, apparently uncon-
cerned with his bad behaviour.

I let him out, showered, then tiptoed downstairs
and filled the dishes as the other animals came wander-
ing in from various parts of the house. It's amazing how
well they can hear! They could be in the deepest sleep
possible, but the second that food hits the first dish,
they're right there.

I took the dogs outside for few minutes, too, going
over their names in my head. There was Plunk, of
course, and Dusty, an old shepherd called Steinbeck,
and a beagle of some description named Boothie.

Steinbeck was the biggest of them and yet I'd seen
Inky — a tiny black cat — washing his ears a couple of
times. It was comical how the big dog just lay there
kind of whimpering and allowed it, even though it was
plain to see he didn't much care for the treatment.

When the dogs had all had a chance to run for a bit
we went back into the house, where I discovered an
orange and white female cat named Sprinkle shoving
against Arthur the Fifth, vying for a place at his dish. I
scooped her up and moved her to a bowl that wasn't
occupied, then went back and gave Arthur a quick pat.
Instead of showing a little appreciation, he gave me a
look that seemed to ask why *I* was bothering him.

Mom came into the kitchen when I had just finished a bowl of cereal. She looked as tired as I felt.

"You're up early."

"Plunk woke me up," I said. "He's such a pest."

"Well, at least you haven't had the pleasure of Rosie's company in the night," she said, a trace of a smile flitting across her face and then disappearing.

"You have?" I asked.

"Well, not by design," she said. "I didn't make my bed yesterday, and when I went to get into it last night, I almost screeched to find Rosie snuggled in under the comforter."

I laughed at the thought but then saw the sad look in Mom's eyes and knew she was thinking of how Rosie had scared Stan that time.

Mom changed the subject and we kept up a conversation for a while, both of us trying to sound normal and cheerful. I wondered if she could see through me as easily as I could see through her. Normally, Mom can sniff out anything phoney inside of three seconds flat, but I don't think she was all that tuned in to what was going on with me at the moment. If she noticed that anything was wrong, she didn't mention it.

It was a relief when the time came to leave for school. I made my way there feeling miserable and only half awake. It wasn't promising to be a very good day!

At least Ashley and Jamie didn't seem to be upset with me over yesterday. Another girl joined us at lunchtime too.

"Hi, I'm Jenna. I'm in Mr. Bittner's class. My brother Jonah is in your class, though." Jenna popped a fry into her mouth and then added, "We're twins," while she chewed it.

"I'm Sarah." That seemed a bit unnecessary. In a school this size, everyone knew who I was.

"Jonah thinks you're cute," Jenna blurted next, watching carefully to see my reaction.

Since I had no idea which of the boys in my class might happen to be Jonah, it was a bit hard to know whether I should be pleased over this announcement or not.

"He sits beside you," Jamie offered helpfully. She held both hands out and glanced at each for a second, concentrating. "On your right."

I could barely picture the boy they were talking about, though I had a vague idea he had dark hair.

"So, you wanna go out with him?" Jenna asked through more fries. I could see them mashing in her mouth, mixed with ketchup and all gross-looking.

I felt like saying that if his manners were anything like hers, I'd pass. Instead, I said, "I don't even know him." I thought that would settle it.

"So, you'll *get* to know him." Her eyes narrowed as she spoke and I could see she wasn't pleased that I hadn't jumped at the chance.

"Well, the truth is," I lied, "I already have a boyfriend. In Ontario."

She shrugged then and let it drop. I thought I'd handled it pretty well, until Ashley cornered me later on.

"Why'd you lie to Jenna?"

"What do you mean?"

"About having a boyfriend in Ontario."

"What makes you think I was lying?" I felt myself squirm as she looked right at me.

"I asked you that the first day you got here. You said no."

I vaguely remembered the onslaught of questions she and Jamie had asked that day.

"I didn't know what else to say," I admitted. "She seemed pretty determined, and I didn't want to say I'd go out with someone I don't know at all."

"You still shouldn't have lied." Ashley seemed really angry.

"I'm sorry. I felt, you know, pressured and stuff."

"At the pool the other day," she said, apparently determined to keep me on the hot seat, "when you said that guy wasn't your mom's boyfriend. Was that a lie too?"

When she asked me that, it seemed that everything from the past few days came crashing down around me. I tried to fight the tears, but they started to come anyway.

"Hey, now," Ashley said, her voice softening, "don't do that. Here, come to the washroom before someone sees you."

When we got there, I found myself telling her the whole story, how I hadn't wanted Stan around at first, and how I'd changed my mind about that and then ruined everything without even meaning to.

"See, lying just causes trouble." Ashley seemed pretty stuck on that theme. "If you'd been honest, none of this would have happened."

I had nothing to say to that. She was right.

"I *hate* lying." Ashley seemed to have drifted off as she spoke. "My mother has a big problem with it. She lies continually, about nothing and everything. Dad says it's a form of mental illness."

"I've heard of that," I said quickly, glad she'd switched to talking about someone else. "It's like some sort of compulsive thing, right?"

"You have no idea. She can't keep a friend because everyone sees what she's like in no time. And imagine what it's like for me and my Dad. We're her own family and we can't believe a word that comes out of her mouth. It's awful."

I understood why she'd reacted the way she had then, though I didn't think there was any similarity between me and Ashley's mom.

All afternoon, I kept thinking about what it would be like to have a mother like that.

CHAPTER TWENTY-THREE

The rest of the week hurried past, and by Saturday Mom seemed to be getting back to normal. She never mentioned Stan, so I guess she must have accepted that was the end of anything that might have been developing between them. I noticed, though, that she spent a lot of time talking about how busy she was going to be with the Hope Chest and how she wouldn't have much time for anything else. Seemed as though she was persuading herself that she didn't have time for him anyway.

David came over at five on Saturday morning to help us with the yard sale, which was advertised to start at seven. He'd already been by on Friday evening and we'd set up tables in the driveway, so it was just a matter of lugging everything out and organizing it. Mom had put price tags on everything with squares of masking tape. We started with the furniture — old-fashioned tables, dressers, wardrobes, and some strange pieces I didn't even know the names for. Then we brought out bags and boxes of smaller stuff.

Our first customers arrived before we were even ready for them, so I got put in charge of the cash box while Mom and David finished getting things set up. By seven o'clock, our official opening time, we'd already had a few dozen people and had sold almost a hundred dollars' worth of small items as well as two pieces of furniture that brought in $350 between them. I was amazed at how excited folks got over some of the things.

The morning flew by in a blur of activity. I couldn't believe how many people came to our sale or how fast the enormous piles of stuff on the tables went down.

By noon, the onslaught of customers had slowed to a trickle and we finally had time to count the money. We'd made almost two thousand dollars! I couldn't believe it, but Mom said she wasn't surprised.

"A lot of the furniture pieces were antique," she explained. "We probably could have gotten more for some of them, but I just wanted to get rid of it all."

Even though we'd sold a tremendous amount of stuff, there was still quite a bit left. Mom was trying to decide what to do with it when a young woman came along pushing a baby in an old-fashioned stroller. It was obvious from the way they were dressed that she was poor.

She walked in slowly and looked over the tables, peeking shyly at us once in a while. A few times she picked something up, but she didn't hang onto anything the way people did when they were going to buy it. She paused for a long time, looking at a big old blender — the kind with a glass top.

"Those are very handy for making baby food," Mom said helpfully.

"Is it really only three dollars?" the woman asked in a tiny, timid voice.

"What's your baby's name?" Mom asked, instead of answering her question about the price.

"This here's Ginny" — a hint of pride crept into her face — "and I'm Allison."

"Well, Allison, I'd love it if you'd take anything you want as our gift to Ginny." Mom smiled. "She's the cutest baby I've seen since my Sarah was that size."

Allison's face flushed with surprise and she didn't speak for a moment. When she did, it was to murmur a hushed thank you. Then she picked up the blender and said she'd like to take it, if Mom was sure it was all right.

"Oh, there must be some other things you could use," Mom said. "I don't think many more people will be showing up, and I just want to get rid of as much stuff as possible. You'd be doing me a favour, honestly."

By the time Mom was finished, Allison had a couple of boxes of things, which we packed and put to one side. Mom got her address and told her we'd send it all over to her place in a taxi.

"That was really nice of you," David said, as we all started putting what hadn't been sold back into boxes.

"You know, David," Mom said, "a few months ago I couldn't afford to give anyone anything. Sarah and I were poor as church mice ourselves. It feels really good to be able to help someone else."

"Stan's like that, too," David went on, unaware of what had happened. "My dad says he's always doing things for people. He said Stan doesn't talk about it, either, just goes and does things. Dad says that counts more than if you help someone and brag about it."

David didn't seem to notice that Mom had gone kind of still and quiet or that she didn't answer. He just went on, talking about a few things that he'd heard Stan had done. I finally caught his eye and shook my head just enough for him to notice. He understood right away and stopped in mid-sentence.

"So, where did you want to put all this stuff?" His voice was awkward as he changed the subject.

"Well, it can't go back where it was," Mom said. "Let's see if there's enough room in the shed out back."

The shed was already half full of garden tools and a bunch of odd-looking junk, but we managed to squeeze the boxes in there. Then Mom paid David for helping, passing him an envelope with money in it. He thanked her and stuck it in his pocked without counting it.

"Want a sandwich?" I asked him, hoping he'd stay a bit longer. He said that would be great, so I threw together some ham and cheese on sunflower flax bread, filled a couple of glasses with lemonade, and brought it all outside. We sat on the front step and ate.

"So, what's up with Stan?" David asked me as he drained the last of his lemonade. "I thought he was going out with your mom."

"Not exactly," I said slowly. "I think things were headed that way, but he hasn't been around for the last week."

"Well, it's none of my business." He shrugged, looking a bit embarrassed.

Then, unbelievably, I found myself telling him the whole story about the towel and pool and bathing cap and what I'd said. Even as I was talking, I knew it was a dumb thing to do. He'd *never* ask me out after hearing what I'd done, not even after I'd turned thirteen. The whole thing was weighing on me, though, and it was a relief to talk about it.

David didn't say anything for a minute after I'd finished, and I was kind of scared he might just get up and walk away in disgust. I knew that Stan was something of a hero to him, so he must have thought I was the biggest jerk ever.

When he finally spoke, it wasn't at all what I'd expected.

"I think I can understand how you must have felt, you know, like everyone thought the wrong way about your mom and all."

"I still messed up bad."

"Yeah, you did. But my gram always says it's okay to make mistakes, so long as you try to make them right."

I asked him how I was supposed to do that, but he said he couldn't help me there and I needed to figure that one out on my own.

It looked as though I was either going to have to admit the whole mess to Mom or learn to live with the guilt. Neither option appealed to me much.

Chapter Twenty-Four

When I went into the house after talking to David, I'd almost made my mind up to confess everything to Mom. I might have, too, except that when I got inside she was on the phone in the living room. As I got to the doorway, she beckoned me over with a big smile on her face.

"Someone would like to speak to you," she said as she passed me the phone.

"Sarah? Is it really you, dear?" My grandmother's voice came through the line as soon as I'd said hello.

"Yes, it's me, Grammie." I almost laughed at her question. Did she think Mom might have put some strange kid on the phone to trick her?

"Your mother tells me that you've made some friends at your new school," Grammie said next.

"A few."

"So, things are going all right there in your new home?"

"Mmm hmm. Pretty good."

"Well, that's great, dear. But you know, your grandfather and I miss seeing you already."

"I miss you too," I said. A sudden lump came in my throat and I had to swallow hard.

"So, we were wondering…"

The big pause tipped me off that something good was coming. Grammie likes to tell things that way, with a dramatic pause and a big finish. I knew whatever she was going to say next would be a surprise for me.

"How would you like to spend the summer here, with us?"

"Wow! That would be awesome, Grammie," I said, excited at the thought of seeing my grandparents and friends and just being back in Ontario.

"Well, your grandfather and I have talked it over and we've decided to fly you here for your summer vacation!"

"The whole thing?" Oddly, I suddenly didn't feel as happy at the thought as you might expect.

"Well, sure, if you want. Or as much of it as you'd like."

"A month would be perfect," I said after only a slight hesitation.

We agreed on that, then I talked to Grampie for a bit before saying goodbye.

"That was a surprise," Mom said after I'd hung up.

"I *know*. And it will be my first time flying, too!"

"Well, that too, but I was surprised you didn't want to spend the whole summer there."

It had shocked me a bit, too. Even though my first reaction was pure excitement, it had been chased almost immediately by other thoughts. Like, Jamie and Ashley and the way we'd become friends so easily and things that might be going on around here — stuff I didn't even know about yet but figured I'd want to. And, of course, there was Mom and her Hope Chest store, and all the animals, and the house, and even David.

I realized, with a bit of a start, that I was already starting to feel as though Miramichi was my home.

"I guess it's sinking in that this house is really ours and our lives are really going to be here," I told Mom.

"And you don't mind as much as you thought you would?"

"I really don't mind at all." Of course, it was easy to feel that way when so many of our circumstances had improved. But there was more to it than that, and it occurred to me that Aunt Sarah's diaries had given the place a special meaning to me.

We had a late dinner that night and talked for a long time about my upcoming visit with my grandparents.

After that, Mom got talking about the Hope Chest, and even though it was more exciting to her than it was to me it seemed to be cheering her up, so I was glad to hear all about her plans, even the boring ones like what colour the curtains would be.

She even brought up how handy it would be to have a car for some of the things she needed to arrange and buy and so on, but she kind of dropped that quick.

That gave me a twinge of guilt again, since Stan had told Mom he'd help her look for a car when she was ready to buy one. I wondered if she was thinking about that too, because she looked down for a few seconds when she mentioned it. Then she lifted her head right back up and smiled in the way you do when you're forcing yourself to look happy.

Even with those little reminders that Mom still felt bad, it was clear that she felt better than she had at first. Maybe Stan was just a passing fancy.

The more I thought about it, the more I convinced myself that it might be best just to let the whole thing go. What good would it do to tell Mom what I'd done? She'd just be mad at me, and it wouldn't change anything. He'd still be gone.

Anyway, how did I know that things would have gone anywhere with them? It wasn't like they were seeing each other for a long time — after all, they barely knew each other. I persuaded myself that it was no big deal after all, that probably nothing would have come of it in any case.

By the time Plunk and Arthur the Fifth and I settled into bed for the night, I'd pretty much decided I wasn't going to think about it any more. I reached for Sarah's journal and was soon reading all about how often Mr. King came to call on her and how she was falling more and more in love with him. I'd read about a dozen entries when I came to one that pushed away my growing sleepiness.

June 16

I have never been angrier in my life! Father has forbidden me to see Mr. King again. Horrid rumours have sprung up regarding a business difficulty in Mr. King's past and as one might expect there are those who are ready to judge without first obtaining a reliable account of the matter. Sadly, father is such a one.

I can only be thankful that Mr. King, on hearing that this talk had arisen, called on me earlier this very day to set my mind at rest.

How my heart went out to him as he laid before me, in anguished detail, a full admission of his past folly. Indeed, his countenance was so distressed when he told me of the treachery he had faced, causing near ruin to himself and others, that I scarce could keep from weeping over his misfortune.

"Sarah, my dearest," he said, "a former partner betrayed both our friendship and the company we shared. While the financial losses were staggering, hardest of all to bear was the knowledge that an upright man had fallen so low. There were those who blamed me as much as him, though I myself had suffered losses greater than any other."

Knowing that fallacious details of this matter have reached father and that he has chosen to believe the worst of my beloved Mr. King is more than I can stand. I tried to explain it all to Father but he would not listen to the truth — that Mr. King's only crime was in trusting a scoundrel.

I long to go to Mr. King, to speak full assurances of my trust and faith. I cannot bear to have him think that I too have come to believe the worst of him and yet I fear it is the only conclusion he can draw when he finds himself unwelcome at our door.

I shall not sleep tonight, so heavy is my heart.

I sat straight up in bed, feeling all the anger and indignation Sarah herself must have felt so many years ago. As questions ran through my mind, my eyes were drawn back to the journal.

June 18

These past two days have been torture but at last I was able to find a way to get a message to my Mr. King.

Burgess Fennel reluctantly agreed to arrange delivery of a letter I'd written and sealed. It was only by taking her into my confidence that I was able to persuade her when she and Eliza were here for afternoon tea.

I must hope earnestly that Burgess will honour her promise to me to keep the matter from Eliza. I fear Eliza would, at the very least, prevent the delivery, or, at worst, bring the matter to my father's attention. It is not that Eliza is a mean person, and I know she would not do it out of spite, but she may from a self-righteous sense of duty.

I fear that I crossed the boundary of ladylike behaviour in my missive to Mr. King. And yet, how could I not? Surely he ought to know what is in my heart.

I blush now to think of my words to him, words declaring my allegiance to him as one would hardly dare speak to a fiancé. Of course, he has made no promise to me of his intentions, but I am nonetheless quite confident that his love for me is as strong and sure as is mine for him.

I felt I had no choice but to express myself frankly and this I did. I told him of the rumours that brought about his banishment from this home and of Father's willingness to believe the worst. Yet, I assured him in every possible way that my own faith *and trust in his integrity is unshaken. I told him that there is no man who is more worthy of these sentiments. And (I blush to confess) I told him my affection for him has not and could not be swayed by libellous gossip.*

As I watched the Fennel carriage carry off the twins, together with my letter, I had a momentary pang of uncertainty. Perhaps Mr. King will find my words too forward, too presumptuous on our short acquaintance. And yet, how can I doubt his affection for me? His words have been only tender, his every action gentlemanlike and solicitous.

No, I am sure he means to make me his wife, and it is only proper that I declare myself to him in his time of adversity.

I closed the diary and held it against my heart, unable to stop the trembling it had caused inside me. Poor, poor Sarah! How could her father have stood in the way of her happiness? His own daughter!

And what had happened with her and Mr. King? Obviously they were in love — and it sure sounded like she was willing to marry him. How was it that she had ended up alone in another province?

Book two surely held the answers to those questions, but it would have to wait for another day. I couldn't focus to read any further that night no matter how much I wanted to know what happened next.

My last thought falling asleep that night was: poor Sarah! How horrible it must all have been for her.

CHAPTER TWENTY-FIVE

By the time another week had gone by I was getting used to the routine of doing my share to take care of the animals and help out around the house but there were still a few jobs I didn't like. Cleaning the litter boxes was one and walking those four silly dogs was another.

Don't get me wrong, I've gotten to the point that I like the pets we inherited okay. It's just that when you're taking the dogs for a walk, half the time they all want to go in different directions and the other half they nearly drag you along the road like you're some kind of limp puppet.

Last week Mom had come up with the idea that if we brushed the cats and dogs every day, they wouldn't shed all over the house so much. It was a real challenge to keep up with the hair, I must admit. We swept the hardwood floors and vacuumed all the carpeting every day, but even so, we just couldn't stay ahead of the problem. Well, brushing didn't make any difference either! It just added one more thing to our growing list of things to do.

Mom doesn't give up easily and she had another idea early this week. She decided we should restrict the cats and dogs to a couple of rooms downstairs.

"Then," she said, all optimistic sounding, "there won't be any hair in the rest of the house and we'll just have to do those two rooms every day."

It was an idea that sounded great and should have worked out perfectly except for the fact that it didn't work at all. We spent five exhausting days leading, prodding, or carrying our furry collection — the cats into the parlour and the dogs into the den. We nearly wore our voices out telling them to "Stay!" or firmly saying "No!" when they started to wander away. Of course, we put up every possible kind of barrier to keep them in, especially at first. Nothing worked. They clawed through cardboard, jumped over and around the different pieces of furniture we tried, and generally seemed to look on overcoming every obstacle as some kind of game. A game that *they* won.

After a few days of that Mom said maybe the right approach wasn't to *trap* them but to *train* them. Hah!

I don't know how Mom coped during the daytime when I was in school. I found it hard enough to keep up with them from around four o'clock when I got home until bedtime, and that was when there were two of us keeping after them.

It's hard to say whether the whole experience was harder on us or on the poor animals. They must have been confused — after having free rein of the place their whole lives — to suddenly have these two lunatics trying to force them to stay in one place.

The cats were just impossible! Any idea we might have had that they were co-operating was just an illusion brought on by the fact that the lazy things would often lie down and nap for a while once we'd got them into their room. However, the very second the urge struck them to go anywhere else in the house, off they went. You could bring them back twenty times and they'd just keep walking away.

The dogs were just as challenging in their own way. I actually felt sorry for the two bigger dogs during this doomed experiment. Unlike the smaller Plunk and Dusty, who trotted off at will with nary a thought in their seemingly empty little heads, Steinbeck and Boothie seemed to be trying to grasp what was going on. They would sit, heads tilted, eyes questioning, tails wagging happily to show their willingness to follow instructions while we (I hate to admit this, but it's true) actually *explained* that we wanted them to stay *here* in *this room*.

The problem was that the instructions never seemed to become clear to them, and after a while they would just wander away, probably hoping that the next directions we gave them would be a bit easier to understand.

There were a lot of confused and frustrated faces, and not just the animals', before Mom threw her hands up and admitted defeat.

"Oh, let the wretched things go wherever they want," she said. "They're beyond training and we're just making things harder on ourselves."

Oddly enough, I felt kind of indignant to hear her call them "the wretched things" like that. They couldn't help shedding or doing things they'd always been allowed to do, and they were, after all, *our* pets.

Well, between that ill-fated project, homework, and chores, I was so tired by bedtime every night that I was asleep almost as soon as I'd settled into bed. As anxious as I was to find out what happened next in Sarah's life, it wasn't until Friday (right after Mom acknowledged defeat) that I had a chance to begin reading the second diary.

I had a quick peek back at the last entries in the first book to refresh my memory and then eagerly took up the next volume to see what happened after Sarah's father had forbidden her from seeing Mr. King again and she had sent him the letter telling him how she really felt.

June 24

Surely this was the longest week of my life! It was barely to be endured. So despondent did I find myself that I could not even find the heart to write. Days without any reply from Mr. King left me to wonder — had he received my letter? And if so, had he looked on it with shock and ill will over its familiarity?

But today! At last a reply has come. First, a note arrived yesterday morning, from Burgess, inviting me to a game of whist this afternoon. The invitation seemed unusually insistent, so I felt sure she had some message for me.

Still, I mentioned it to Mother in the most idle manner, as though it interested me not in the least. Any display of eagerness or enthusiasm would have raised her suspicions. Instead, she was insistent that I should go (as I knew she would be), doubtless thinking it would make an excellent distraction from my thoughts of Mr. King.

I had no opportunity to speak with Burgess alone until we had finished the first hands and paused for refreshments. Even then, she managed to be subtle.

"Do try one of these," she said, holding out a tray of iced cakes. At the same time she passed me a napkin, which she glanced at very quickly.

I took it with trembling hand, meeting her eye with the slightest nod, and felt at once the stiffness of a letter hidden in its folds.

The question of how to remove the letter unobserved was my single difficulty, and one that I managed as though subterfuge has been a normal part of my life. I simply pretended that a sneeze was impending and stepped out into the hallway with my napkin held up to my nose.

Was I not clever? It took but a few seconds to remove the letter and secure it in the deep pocket on my skirt. The torturous part of the ordeal was waiting until I returned home before I could read it.

And now that I have seen its contents, how happy I am! I am sure that in all of Canada there has never been a happier girl. Mr. King has expressed his love and intention to make me his wife.

Of course, the matter cannot be settled so simply as that. Father will never give his consent, and this was plain to my darling, beloved Mr. King.

What he has proposed is enough to send thrills of fear and delight through me all at once. He will come for me on the afternoon of this coming Thursday! I am to walk along the river until I reach the old road, where he will meet me at about two o'clock. From there (my heart quickens with excitement at the thought) we will travel to Montreal, where we shall be wed and take a short holiday as Mr. & Mrs. Alexander King before returning to Brockville as husband and wife.

I cannot bear to think of what Father and Mother will say when they discover what I have done, but by that time it will, at least, be too late for them to prevent me from the path I am meant to walk.

And, anyway, I am sure they will come to love him even as I have, and when those evil rumours are proven false, everything will be grand.

Oh! I knew that I was destined for something more than a housewife's lot, and it is so! I shall be the wife of the most important businessman ever seen in these parts. As such, it will be my lot to help to bring about change in the affairs of women hereabouts; a role I shall not take lightly but will use for the advancement and betterment of Canadian women so far as my influence may reach.

I was almost as excited as Sarah must have been when she wrote this — except I knew something must have happened to prevent her from her plan to go away and marry Mr. King. As tired as I was, I couldn't put down the diary.

I read several more entries, all filled with plans and happy anticipation. The last of those was written on the morning of the Thursday Mr. King was to come for her, and she promised to write more that evening, but the next entry wasn't until the following day.

June 30

Patience! I must develop patience if I am to be a proper wife to a man of Mr. King's standing in the community. Surely there will be many times when my duty will be to wait for his return from attending to important matters.

Still, it is difficult to be patient when I so long to be at his side. How hard it was to accept the change in plans (as he had intended them) and instead to travel alone to Montreal, where I now wait in solitude for him to join me.

Even more distressing is the delay this will cause in getting word to Mother and Father, who must be frantic with worry over my absence. I had expected to send them word straightaway after our vows had been made and not to leave them anxious on my account for more than a day or two.

I implored Mr. King to send them word but he insisted it was unwise and suggested it would throw our plans to marry into jeopardy. It is true, as he insisted, that someone could be engaged to follow him in order to determine my whereabouts, but surely this would not be attempted if the matter were to be properly studied.

Indeed, the only possible way I can now return with dignity to Brockville is on my husband's arm. Anything less would so tarnish my name that it would be unthinkable to Father.

As it is, every day that passes while I wait is more fodder for the gossip mill.

But I must not think of these things! I must think only of the day (within the fortnight, he promises) when my darling will come to make me his wife, and all shall be glorious and well!

Unable to keep my eyes open another minute, I set the diary aside and clicked off my lamp. Even so, it was hard to fall asleep with the troubling thoughts that were running through my mind.

Clearly, something had gone wrong with the plans that Mr. King and Sarah had made.

CHAPTER TWENTY-SIX

If it had been up to me, I'd have done nothing all day Saturday except read Sarah's diaries. Of course, it wasn't up to me. Mom had her usual ideas about us cleaning the house and me getting my homework out of the way. I have to say, though, that it was still a big improvement over sitting alone in our apartment back in Ontario while she put in her usual shift at Pete's.

Mom had been working away at the Hope Chest (I'd begun thinking of it that way, instead of as the servants' quarters) and she'd already made a lot of progress. Except for the walls being in bad shape — mostly from being banged with stuff that was stored out there — and the fact that it really needs new windows, it was coming along pretty good.

Mom had called a few contractors last week to get prices on the work the place needed inside and on some new windows. We were both stunned when the estimates came in the mail, one on Wednesday and the other on Friday. For just the windows *alone*, the companies she'd contacted wanted more than twice the amount Stan had quoted for the *entire job*.

Their prices for the inside work were just as shocking. To have the walls replaced and display shelves and tables built was going to cost almost seven thousand dollars. It was awful to see Mom sitting at the kitchen table staring at the quotes. It was like she was watching her dream slide away from her.

The bottom line was that if she went ahead with the work, it would take almost half of the money she'd inherited from her great-aunt. I knew she'd never take a risk that big. Besides, she'd told me we'd need most of it to live on while the business got going.

I had the extra guilt of knowing she'd never call Stan to see if he'd still do the work for her. So it was a huge surprise that Saturday when a stranger drove up in an old green half-ton truck and knocked on our kitchen door.

"Afternoon, ma'am. Stan Reynolds sent me to unload these here windows he promised to ya," he explained, pointing to them in the back of the truck. "Said you could let me know if you still wanted the work done at the price he gave you. Me and the boys can start on Monday if you do."

I saw Mom struggling with her pride for a few seconds, but the reality of our situation was strong, and after a moment she smiled and told him she'd sure appreciate it. I saw the wistful look on her face then too, and I knew she'd been covering her disappointment over the way things had ended so suddenly.

I also saw the way her eyes lit up a little when the man reached into his shirt pocket, pulled out a piece of paper, unfolded it, and held it out to her, saying, "Stan said to give you this."

The spark faded when he continued. "Anything you want to know, you can ask me — or let me know if it don't suit. We can change it before we start if there's anything."

She took the paper and studied it a bit, then nodded and told him it was fine just as it was. She offered the sketch back but he waved it away, assuring her Stan would send a more detailed work order with the men when they came to do the job. I noticed that she folded it real gentle and slipped it into her jeans' pocket. It seemed like I knew why she did that, and a pain started up in the pit of my stomach.

To make things worse, she said this called for a celebration and we were going to eat out. So we walked over a nearby restaurant called the Cunard, for

Chinese food, which I love but have had only a few times in my life.

Mom ordered moo goo guy pan while I had a combo plate with sweet and sour chicken balls, fried rice, and chicken chow mein. It was all delicious but I still had a hard time eating.

See, even though things had suddenly turned around, I really didn't feel much better. I tried to persuade myself that the main thing was she'd be able to have her business. I made silent promises to help around the house more and even be cheerful about it. And I told myself she'd meet someone else, that in fact she'd probably meet someone better than Stan. (That actually made me feel worse, like I'd just repeated the whole scene at the pool in a different way.)

You'd think that it would get easier to push the whole thing out of my mind as time passed, but it didn't. If anything, it felt like the guilt was piling itself up higher and higher.

Every time I looked at Mom I saw the shadow of hurt and disappointment and I couldn't escape the fact that I'd caused it. She had to be wondering, after things started out so great between them, what had happened. Did she figure that Stan just decided she was boring or unappealing or — well, who knows what she thought.

I wished I could just tell her it wasn't *her* but there was no way to do that without confessing everything, and somehow it just seemed too late for that. Maybe if I'd spoken up right when it happened, or even a week ago … but two weeks had gone by and it seemed that any chance to talk about it had slid out of reach.

So I just kept trying to push it down and to be extra helpful around the house and I kept trying to persuade myself that if I did enough, I'd have made up for it. Except it didn't seem like something I could even out, no matter what, and it was just eating at me and eating at me.

I tell you, after carrying it around for weeks I was willing to do anything — anything, that is, but tell Mom what I'd done — to make it right. Only I couldn't figure out what that anything might be.

Mom broke into my thoughts as I was thinking all of this. I guess it took her a few tries, because I suddenly realized she'd said my name a couple of times.

"Huh?"

"Goodness, where were you off to?" She smiled now that she'd finally gotten my attention. "Anyway, I was saying that I'm going to go ahead and look for a car. Now that things are really happening with the Hope Chest, there are lots of details I need to take care of, and I can't do any of that without a vehicle."

She paused and smiled and added, "So, anyway, wish me luck! I'm going to try to find one by next week."

Even though we'd talked about getting a car before it had always seemed far away. The thought of having one as early as the coming week was exciting, and I pleaded with Mom to take me with her when she went car shopping.

"Sorry, no can do," she said. "I'll have to go while you're in school."

I opened my mouth to ask why we couldn't go together right after school, but I shut it again quick, remembering my plan to argue less.

"Don't worry," Mom said, "I'll try to pick out something that's cool."

"I know you will, Mom." I forced a smile with the words. "You have great taste. And it will be awesome to actually have our very own car."

"Yes, it will." Her voice and eyes seemed suddenly far away. "You know, Sarah, things are better for us than they've ever been. We have a lot to be thankful for. A lot. We need to be grateful for that and not think about what we're missing."

And the way she said it, the hollow sound of it, like she was trying to convince both of us, brought back the day she'd told me she was lonely. I nearly ran from the room in tears.

CHAPTER TWENTY-SEVEN

It seemed that the only thing that completely distracted me from my nagging conscience was reading Sarah's diaries, and I was only too happy to crawl into bed that night (yes, with my usual companions) and open book two to the next entry.

I'd asked Mom earlier what a fortnight was, remembering that Sarah had written how Mr. King had promised that their wedding would take place within that length of time. Mom wasn't sure, so we'd looked it up together and found out it was two weeks.

I guess that probably didn't seem like very long to Mr. King, but I had a feeling they were the longest weeks of Sarah's life.

Sarah's next few entries were much like the last one I'd read. They gave me a picture of her as a young woman, pacing day after day in her hotel room, waiting for word from her fiancé, waiting to become his wife.

The first sign of a problem came more than a week after her arrival in Montreal.

July 07

So heavy is my heart that I can barely think straight to write. And yet I must, for it seems this diary has become my only solace and friend these past days. To think that I almost burned my journals in the fireplace before leaving home, rather than concealing them in my skirt and bringing them with me.

I grow faint with worry and despair that something has happened to prevent my dearest Mr. King from contacting me. He promised faithfully to send word (as well as additional funds for my lodging and meals) as immediately as possible. Each day that passes is a nightmare of dragging moments, ticking away into tortured hours, and each night a restless suspension of hope.

The hotel manager begins to look at me with unease and yesterday asked if Mademoiselle wished to make some payment toward her account. Mademoiselle most assuredly did not wish any such thing, but fearing I should be turned out into the street, I gave him all but three dollars of what I had in my possession. This did not quite pay my account up to date, but it satisfied him for the moment at least. I doubt another full week will pass before I am asked again for payment.

Mr. King gave me a sum of money when he paid my fare and put me on the train, but it was not enough to last past a week. Of course he meant to send more at once.

I don't suppose it helps my situation that I have but two dresses in my possession. No doubt this has been noted by the staff, who must wonder how someone can afford to stay in a hotel and yet own only two frocks. It is just fortunate that I was able to layer two gowns in a manner that did not show or I should be here with but one.

Or perhaps it is not so fortunate at all. If Mother had noticed anything odd about my attire, if she had discovered the second dress, she would surely have prevented me from leaving the house and I would still be home in my beloved room.

But there is no point to such thoughts. I am here and that is that.

I am fearful now of taking my meals in the hotel dining hall and billing them to my room, as I have done previously. I fear this can only afford the manager more cause to be concerned about payment and I have nothing to offer should he request another deposit toward the balance.

At the same time (though my appetite is waning) I must eat. With the little money I have left I can manage a loaf of bread and a pint of milk each day, but if Mr. King does not soon appear or send word, I fear I shall be in desperate circumstances indeed.

July 09

Oh wretched luck! Today as I returned from my walk, wherein I had secured my food for the day, I encountered a street urchin who clutched at my leg and begged me most piteously to give him a piece of bread. I did this gladly, moved to compassion by the hunger in his eyes.

But the horrid child meant only to rob me, and this he did as soon as I had loosed the grasp on my pocketbook in order that I might tear him off a portion of my loaf. He was gone — disappeared down an alley before I could catch my wits enough to cry out for help.

I returned to the hotel more downcast in spirit than I have ever been. Even so, I checked with the desk perchance something had arrived at last (Mais non, Mademoiselle, nothing today) and came to my room with my bread and milk.

There remains little hope that Mr. King will come to me. Whatever has happened to prevent him must be serious indeed, though I struggle not to think of what ill might have befallen him. I know only that he would be here if he could.

What shall become of me remains a question without answer. I cannot return to Brockville to bring disgrace upon my family and, clearly, I cannot remain here (although I am loath to go perchance Mr. King somehow escapes whatever keeps him from me and makes his way here after all). I fear I shall be forced to sneak away in the night, like some criminal.

But where shall I go? And how shall I live?

July 12

The last of my bread was gone yesterday noon. I had meant to save some small bit of it for later in the day but I could not. Strangely, rising this morning and knowing there was naught to eat was less torturous than yesterday, when the thought of the last dried piece of bread tormented me steadily until I fell on it and ate it like some ravenous bird.

I have spent the day trying to ignore the hunger that gnaws at me. Earlier, I took a walk along the river where I encountered a happy couple lunching on cold chicken and bread and cheese. The sound of their voices, low and murmuring, then light and full of laughter, made me want to flee. But I waited, standing a short way off, pretending to be watching something on the water. I prayed and hoped that they would leave behind some morsel, but they did not.

Tonight I shall leave the hotel, creeping away like some thief. It occurred to me, as I prepared a note for the hotel manager, promising that I would write to make arrangements to settle my account as soon as I am able, that I am giving up more than just a room in which to lay my head at the end of the day.

For the shortest of times this has been my home — at first a happy one. Now, leaving this temporary sanctuary, I must go forth without connection to anyone or anything in the world.

I feel as though my very soul has been set adrift.

I found myself swallowing hard and then brushing tears off my face as I carefully put in a bookmark to mark my place and closed the diary.

I wasn't sleepy but I couldn't bear to continue reading. If things had worked out okay, Sarah's whole life would have been different, so I knew that there was more bad news to come. I just didn't feel like I could face any more tonight.

CHAPTER TWENTY-EIGHT

One day, when there was an unexpected knock at the door, I saw a little flash of hope cross Mom's face. It was gone in a second but I knew what it meant and the nagging voice that I'd been trying to get rid of started up a bit louder again.

I swung the door open thinking how nice it would be if it could just be Stan — if nothing had happened and he was just dropping by and everything was the way it had been before I'd opened my big mouth and said those mean things at the pool.

Of course, it wasn't Stan. It was Allison, the lady with the baby, though Ginny wasn't with her this time.

"I made it for you myself," I heard her say, "to thank you."

She was holding out the prettiest doll I've ever seen. It was all made of cloth, with a ruffled dress and apron. An old-fashioned bonnet was perched on its head, and the face was so cute I wanted to take and hug it.

"Why, Allison, this is beautiful!" Mom wasn't exaggerating, either. "I've never seen anything quite like it."

"I been making them for a while," Allison said, blushing at the compliment. "Ginny has a whole bunch, though she don't play with them much yet."

"All sewn by hand" — Mom seemed to be talking to herself — "and so original. How long does it take you to make one?"

"It's pretty slow, 'cause my sewing machine don't work no more, but I used to be able to finish one in a couple of hours before it broke. The man said it would cost fifty dollars to fix." She paused, and added, "I just use old clothes people give me for them."

The next thing I knew, Mom was asking Allison if she would be interested in making dolls to sell at the Hope Chest.

"We'll get your sewing machine fixed right away, and you can pay me back when you sell some dolls," Mom went on after Allison eagerly agreed to the plan. "People will be happy to pay twenty-five to forty dollars each for these, depending on the size."

After she'd left, I noticed that Mom seemed happier than she had since Stan stopped coming around. It always makes Mom feel good to do something for someone else, though it didn't used to happen often. Before Great-Aunt Sarah died, *we* were usually the ones who needed help.

There's a line Mom used to quote once in a while, from a play or something, that talks about depending on the kindness of strangers. It was one she used whenever someone did something to help us out or gave us something, and for some reason, she always said it with a southern accent.

That night, curled up in bed with Sarah's diary, I discovered that someone had befriended and helped *her*, too. The next entry was more than a month after the one written in July, when she'd been on the verge of sneaking out of the hotel.

August 27

How much has happened since my last entry! It may be just as well that I had no writing implement for some weeks and could not record the misery of the past month and a half. Perhaps writing of the shame and degradation would have been the impetus needed to put into action one of the dark temptations that haunted my every moment. Those dreadful days when walking into the mighty river often seemed as happy a solution as any.

Hunger, and oft-times thirst, had become my constant companions. I slept beneath empty old buildings, begged pennies for food, and struggled to escape the clutches of men and women whose hearts are full of darkness and evil.

One day I ate discarded heads of fish from the garbage at a seafood restaurant. Another, I found myself trembling with jealousy for the marrow in a bone being eaten by a large dog. Every moment hunger consumed me, made its demands, caused me to sink ever lower.

A man offered me a fine meal one day if I should accompany him to his lodgings and, God help me, I may have gone but for the fear that he would either murder me or fail to make good on his promise of food. Such horrors as I never dreamed existed were, for a mercifully short time, my world.

But it is past now. I have left the nightmare behind — but I have also left behind much that was good and worthy.

Alas, Mr. King has proven to be neither of those. Rather, he is a charlatan and a thief. I learned this yesterday when I received a reply to the first letter I was finally able to send to my family. It brought tears to my eyes for many reasons, one of which was discovering for what manner of man I placed myself in such straits.

Mother wrote that he had taken the townsfolk's investments and tried to flee. I shudder to think that he almost certainly intended to meet me with his ill-gotten gains. How thankful I am that he was apprehended before he could make good his escape, for what I have been through would pale in comparison to finding myself the wife of a gangster.

It seems that the people of Brockville were not his first victims, for under a variety of aliases, Mr. King has robbed others in like manner using equally persuasive schemes. He is nothing more than a confidence man.

It occurs to me that I do not even know his real name. How easily I allowed myself to be persuaded by his charm and good looks! What a fool I have been.

I must tell myself very firmly that what has happened is over and done, as Mrs. Taylor, my kind benefactress, has reminded me on more than one occasion.

I met this good woman during one of my darkest moments. I had fainted in the street and she, passing by, called out to her driver to stop. When she learned that I was not ill but starving, she insisted on taking me to a nearby café, where she ordered us a lunch of a thick, creamy soup, sandwiches of cold beef tongue, and tea.

While we ate, we talked, and I found myself telling her the whole story of my foolhardy descent into the sad state in which she found me.

Having learned that I was born and raised a gentlewoman, Mrs. Taylor then told me that if I was willing to accompany her to New Brunswick, she was in a position to help. It had just fallen to her to find a replacement for a departing schoolteacher. I accepted the offer most eagerly and she made arrangements for me to join her party for the journey.

Once here, a family in Chatham agreed to provide me with room and board. They are a sensible couple and not prone to prying, for which I am thankful.

I shall put aside every possible penny of my earnings — first to repay my account at the hotel and my travel expenses to Mrs. Taylor. After that I shall continue to save toward a home of my own. Perhaps when my inheritance comes to me I shall have enough to manage it. After my dreadful ordeal on the streets of Montreal, my only wish is for security.

I have no fear of what lies ahead. I shall hereafter be satisfied and content with my present lot and waste no time on regrets for all I have lost.

One thing is sure. Never again will I place my trust in a man, nor risk my heart. The suffering of this past while has been sufficient for my liking and I shall not chance it again.

I felt this huge sadness to think of Sarah living her life alone out of fear that someone else would hurt her. Whether or not she had ever felt differently, she had chosen to remain on her own for the rest of her life.

How horrible to be so hurt and scared that you give up. Mom always says people deserve a second chance, but Sarah hadn't given herself one.

I lay there thinking about so many things that my head started to hurt. The events of the day and the past few weeks all swam together until it was all a jumbled mess.

But the final thoughts that came to me before I fell asleep were about second chances. And just as I drifted away, I knew what I had to do.

CHAPTER TWENTY-NINE

By the time school was over the next day, my stomach was all tied up in knots over what I'd decided to do. It sure wasn't going to be easy, but my mind was made up.

The more I'd thought about telling Mom about what had happened at the pool, the more I'd realized that wasn't the solution. She'd be upset to find out I'd been rude after Stan had done so much to help us. Of course, she might also feel a bit better, knowing he hadn't just lost interest in her, but she wouldn't *do* anything. That's not her style.

So, telling Mom wouldn't *fix* anything, and *that* was what I wanted to do — if it wasn't too late. The only question was when I'd get a chance to carry out my new plan. I have to admit part of me was hoping something would come up to delay it.

Have you ever noticed that when there's something you aren't exactly looking forward to doing, it's really easy to find reasons to put it off? I'd have taken just about any excuse to buy myself time, but I couldn't find one.

My mind was already made up that I wouldn't do it when Mom was around, even if she was in another part of the house. I didn't want her to know anything about it, at least, not just yet.

Well, when I walked into the kitchen, the first thing I saw was a note on the table. The message was brief — and had obviously been written in excitement, since Mom's usually neat writing was scrawled sloppily.

"Sarah, I've gone to finalize things and pick up OUR CAR! Be ready to go for a drive when I get back! Love, Mom."

She could come home any minute, I rationalized. Maybe I should wait until some other time when I knew how long she was going to be gone.

Coward! my conscience screeched. Do it and get it over with.

It's not always easy to argue with your conscience, mainly because it's usually pointing out the truth. I took a deep breath, got the phone book out, and turned to the names starting with *R*.

I found Stan's number right away, walked quickly to the phone, and dialled it before I could change my mind.

It had rung three times, and I was just starting to hope no one was home, when he answered.

"Hello?"

"Uh, hi. Is this Stan?"

"Sure is." I could picture him nodding as he answered.

"This is Sarah." My mouth had gone suddenly dry. "Sarah Gilmore."

There was silence for a few seconds, and the thought flashed through my mind that he might just hang up. Then he spoke.

"Sarah. Well, how are you?"

"I'm fine." That wasn't exactly true, since my knees were starting to shake and I was nervous as could be. Still, it didn't seem the kind of thing I'd want to tell him.

"Well, good. That's great. I'm glad to hear it."

There was another pause, only this time I was the one having a hard time finding something to say. I swallowed and forced myself to speak before it got too awkward.

"I wanted to explain, you know, about that day at the pool."

"I see."

"Actually, I wanted to apologize for what I said." This wasn't going the way I'd pictured it. It was a lot harder. "See, the kids were saying rude stuff about my mom, and it got me upset. I know that's no excuse, but I wanted you to know that I didn't mean what I said about you. I was just trying to shut them up. About my mom."

"I guess I can understand that," Stan said.

"So, I was hoping that you could forgive me, and that you'd still be friends with my mom."

"How *is* your mom?"

"She's fine. Well, I mean, she's all right, but I think she misses you."

"What makes you say that?"

"I can tell. You were the first friend she made here, and I know she liked having you around. I did too."

"Have you told your mother about what happened?"

"Not yet, but I'm going to when she gets home. She's not here right now. I know I should have told her before, because she's been wondering why you stopped coming around. It was bothering me so much, and I didn't know what to do. Then I realized that I had to tell you I was sorry, even if you never want to come here again."

"I'm glad you called, Sarah. I guess it wasn't easy for you. And I like your mom very much but I didn't want to get between the two of you. Your comment at the pool made me think there was a problem developing. Seemed best for me to step out of the picture."

"Because you thought I didn't want you around?"

"Well, yes. I had to consider your feelings."

"So, maybe, now that you know I didn't mean what I said, you'll come over again sometime?" I said.

"Well, I think it would be best to leave that up to your mother," he said.

When we'd finished talking and I hung up the phone, I felt this huge relief. It had been hard to call, but I felt so much better that it seemed foolish I hadn't done it sooner. Now that it was over with, I could hardly wait for Mom to get home. Even though telling her wouldn't be any easier, I was actually looking forward to it.

I didn't have long to wait. Mom drove in about fifteen minutes after I'd talked to Stan. She was pretty excited about her car, which was natural since it was the first one she'd ever owned. Grampie used to let her use his once in a while for something important, but that wasn't the same.

"Are you ready to go for a drive?" she asked after we'd admired it together for a few minutes. "I thought maybe we'd celebrate by eating out tonight."

I was tempted to wait until later to tell her about Stan and almost persuaded myself that it would be a shame to ruin her happy mood. Then my conscience started bugging me again.

"There's something I need to talk to you about first," I said.

I guess my voice and the expression on my face told her it was serious because she walked straight into the house, set the car keys down on the kitchen table, plunked herself into a chair, and waited.

Believe it or not it was easier to tell her, partly because I wasn't as nervous and partly because after talking to Stan the whole thing didn't seem so horrible and hopeless.

She sat there quietly while I told her what had happened. I'd expected her to get angry but mainly she just looked solemn, and when I finished she nodded.

"So *that's* why Stan doesn't come here anymore," she said. There was relief in her voice and I realized that she was almost happy about it. Not about what I'd done, but that she knew Stan hadn't just decided she wasn't his type or whatever.

"It was all my fault. I'm *really* sorry," I said.

"Well, it's over and done with now," she said. Her voice had gotten quiet again and I suddenly realized I hadn't told her everything.

"I called him," I said.

"You *did*?" Her eyes widened a little. "When?"

"A little while ago, just before you got home."

"And what did you say to him?"

"I explained what happened and told him I didn't mean what I said at the pool. And I told him I was sorry."

She didn't say anything but there was a question on her face. I knew right away what she was wondering.

"Oh, and I asked him if he might want to come over again sometime. He said he thought he should leave that up to you."

"Up to me?"

"Yeah. So you should call him and invite him over."

"I don't know." Mom looked as uncertain as her voice sounded. "It would be pretty awkward after all this time has passed. Perhaps it's best just to let things be."

Chapter Thirty

I thought it would be easy to persuade Mom to call Stan, but it wasn't. I got wondering if maybe I'd been mistaken about how bad she'd felt about the whole thing. When she didn't call him that day or the next I decided that I'd done what I could, but this was something that just couldn't be repaired.

But then, on Thursday, just as I was putting away the dishes after dinner, I heard a car pull into our driveway. I looked out the window and saw Stan getting out of it and I got a strange, happy lurch inside me.

"Stan's here," I said to Mom, just as casual as could be.

She got flustered, I could see it, but she stood there with her hands holding onto each other and her chin up, facing the door as I swung it open.

"Hello, ladies." He smiled uncertainly. "I thought I'd check on how things are going with your renovations. Make sure it's all being done as you wanted and whatnot."

"Yes, it's all fine. Wonderful, in fact." Mom smiled back, her nervousness matching his. Her face was getting a bit pink.

"I'd like to have a quick look at it if you don't mind," Stan said. "Make sure my crew is on schedule and all." He hadn't nodded once, and for some strange reason I found myself wishing he would.

"Of course," Mom said. She turned and walked ahead of him as they went out to the Hope Chest.

They were out there for a while and I was itching to know what was happening. When they came back into the kitchen, though, my first reaction was disappointment. They were just talking about the work that was being done, and the awkwardness was still there between them.

"Well," Stan said, "it looks as though everything is under control, all right. They should be finished this week and then you'll be ready to roll. Just give me a call if anything doesn't suit."

Mom told him thank you very much and yes she would but she was sure everything would be fine.

Stan nodded then — first time — and said he wished Mom the best with her business and all. Then he said good night.

So Mom said good night, too. But then, just as he was pulling the door open, she said, "Maybe you'd like a cup of coffee before you go."

And Stan said coffee would be real nice.

I finished reading the last of Sarah's diaries the next week. By then, of course, I'd come to understand what she meant when she'd left the message that "everything that matters is in the chest."

The rest of the second diary pretty much talked about getting used to living in a new place and what it was like to teach at the school. There was a sad, wistful tone to almost every sentence, somehow, and I knew she was missing her home and family.

One surprise was an entry she made a few months after she'd settled in.

November 02

The winter will soon be upon us and I am told that it can be harsh and unforgiving in this part of the country. Of course, I am accustomed enough to snow and cold, and Mother was kind enough to send my belongings by train, so I have plenty of warm clothing for the season.

How grand my things looked to me when I first opened the crates and saw them again. And yet, I suddenly found that I was sobbing uncontrollably and could not stop. Thankfully, there was no one about to hear me.

It seemed the saddest thing in the world to me that these things are all that is left to me of my former life. My family, my friends, are forever lost, as are those familiar houses and sounds. I shall never again hear my mother singing low as she works her needle or my father clearing his throat as he is about to offer thanks for our food.

How I wish I had spent more time with Richard and Stephen, talked to them more, learned what they dream and hope and believe. It seems that our time together was wasted entirely, and that my own brothers are strangers to me in many ways.

It is too late. Too late to walk the paths and sit by the streams, or breathe in the sweet scent of the fields after a rain, or feel the sun on my face while my feet stand on the land where I was born.

Too late to see the value that I missed in so much around me. What I would give to know again the dear company of Mr. Colby, to sit and listen to his honest dreams. I think, perhaps, had I the chance, that his affection may seem more worthy to me now.

Ah, but Mother's latest letter tells me that he will marry Felicity Corcoran in the spring. I hope they will be happy.

Her third diary was written in random entries over the next nine years, with a surprise at the very end (which

I shall save for the moment). By then she was mainly writing if there was something significant to report, like receiving her inheritance or buying her first home or even getting her first cat. The brief notes about other things told me that she enjoyed teaching and very much liked the children, but there is no mention as to whether she ever wished she'd had a child of her own.

It was not clear to me, though I read every word she had written, whether or not Sarah ever truly found the contentment she had hoped for when she first came to New Brunswick.

There was no mention of anyone in her family visiting her or of her returning to her hometown of Brockville. She recorded each of parents' deaths with only a simple notation of the details followed by the words, "Rest in the Lord."

It seemed to me that her entries grew more and more emotionless, and I thought that perhaps she had stopped keeping a diary altogether, not because there weren't things happening in her life, but because she cared too little about them to bother recording them.

The most surprising thing of all was coming to the last entry in the final book and finding the ink newer and brighter than all previous entries. When I read it, I realized why.

Dear Sarah,

I'm an old woman now, and foolish, so when I tell you how pleased I am that your mother named you after me, you'll just have to go along with it.

Someday, if you have taken the time to read through these journals, you will become the first and only family member to fully know my story. Probably, in this day and age, it seems much less shocking than it did years ago, but if you've any brain at all you'll understand nevertheless. (And if you've no brain, it's most unlikely that you've read far enough to see these words, so I needn't fear offending you.)

Well! I'm sorry we never met. I would have liked that, but I long ago came to a place where I just let things happen instead of trying to make them happen.

The world has changed a good deal since I looked at it with the eyes of youth, but I'll warrant there are two things that haven't changed at all. One of them is love, and the other one is heartbreak. You can't open a book or watch a television show or talk to a neighbour without hearing about one or the other or both.

I've learned at last that one will never prevent the other unless we let it. And that should never be.

Live your life, child.

With love,
Sarah Wentworth

It wasn't a sad message, but as I closed the diary I found tears welling up in my eyes and spilling down my cheeks. I felt, somehow, as though I'd known Aunt Sarah, as if we'd spent long afternoons on the veranda drinking lemonade and talking.

I'd never known her and yet it seemed that I did. There, in the old hope chest, she'd managed to somehow leave me ... well, herself!

I thought then of the contents of the hope chest, the hand-embroidered pillowslips and doilies, and something occurred to me. All of the items in there had been old except for one: the lavender quilt. And I somehow *knew* that Aunt Sarah had made that in her later years, that she had painstakingly sewn each stitch by hand — for me.

I went to the hope chest then, lifted the quilt out, and unfolded it for the first time. There, in the centre, circled by ladies with parasols, skilfully embroidered in dark gold thread, was my full name. Sarah May Gilmore.

I knew I would treasure it always, just as I would treasure its giver.